DEAD SHOCK

A SCIFI HORROR NOVEL (SHOCK SERIES, EPISODE I)

WALLACE HENRY

JOIN THE NEWSLETTER!

SERIAL KILLERS. ELDER GODS. ALIEN POLITICIANS.
MONSTERS. SPACE ZOMBIES. HEAVY METAL CULTS.

Chances are, if it's scary, spooky, or disgusting, it's going to end up in one of my books.

Join the newsletter to get a FREE prequel novella to my first novel, 'The Playroom.'

https://mailchi.mp/a2684c1d9318/playroom

1

It was supposed to be a routine contact mission for the UG, a way of keeping tabs on an oppressed population aboard a rogue ship.

But because momentum often carries good intentions beyond their use, this mission became something else entirely.

A nightmare, maybe.

Then again, no one knew that at first.

Approaching the spacecraft, nothing looked amiss. There was a murderous, tyrannical dictator aboard, but that had been true as long as there had been ships floating through the vastness of space.

The UG—United Galaxy—spent ninety percent of its time and energy maintaining intergalactic cooperation among the ships that once had been countries on Earth, and someone or another was perpetually involved in deviant, deeply undiplomatic behavior.

Alejandro Guerra, the resident peace officer aboard, was under the distinct and unwavering impression that he would be landing for a quick look-see and then reporting back to his superiors. It was his first of these, and he intended on making it the cornerstone of his career.

Their ship, The Arumishi, was equipped with weapons of aggression, but he was so confident they wouldn't be needed that he had kept them—well, most of them—locked in the armory for safe keeping.

The weapons, if needed, fired blasts of kinetic energy to dispel riots and tamp down bloody insurgencies.

What most people did not know was that, if placed on a high enough setting, the weapons could entirely dismember a human being with a single blast.

But Guerra did not anticipate such a display of aggression. This was a diplomatic mission, after all, and Guerra himself was not accustomed to anything but peaceable endeavors.

The youngish diplomat blinked, trying to rid his mind of the horrors found in the briefing materials. He was standing on the bridge, leaning forward and watching the ship, their ultimate destination, get bigger with each passing moment.

The entire crew was there with him, all holding its collective breath.

"They're not answering," Cap said from his place among the controls. "I know our comms are working, so why the radio silence?"

The Captain, or Cap—that was all anybody ever called him—was a scruffy man with a face made red and puffy from alcoholism. He was grim-faced and gravel-voiced, but he was damned good at his job.

Aiden, Cap's second-in-command, looked from the ship's main driver to Guerra and then shrugged. He was seldom seen and even more seldom heard, but he was good at his job and Captain seemed to like it that way.

Guerra cleared his throat. Being the ostensible leader here—though he felt far from it—he was tempted to say something.

Thankfully, Aiden saved him the embarrassment. He felt like a teacher on the first day of Academy, trying to set the tone for the mission but clueless as to how to go about it.

"I'll make second contact," Aiden said, his voice as clear and fresh as his face. He was bold and competent and would, no doubt, pilot his own ship someday in the coming years.

He tried again and received only static in return.

Appearing in the space between Cap and Aiden was a kid barely out of his teens. Sterling wore the outfit of the UG, but everything about him appeared counterfeit, in part because everyone thought his rich old man had bribed his way into the organization. To be an officer in the UG was a springboard to more substantive political ambitions.

"That's odd," the kid said, looking down at the ship, his voice a quavering mess. He sounded as terrified as he looked. "Is that a bad sign? Are we in any kind of danger?"

Katarina, the soldier, only blinked. "We're *always* in a kind of danger," she said. "Now act accordingly."

Guerra was unperturbed. He'd been studying up on the ARK, and this sort of rule-bending and out-and-out defiance was...typical of the leader and his people. They seemed to derive a perverse kind of pleasure at thumbing their nose at the main deliberative body in the galaxy.

"Maybe they think we'll turn around," Guerra said. "They've sidestepped sanctions from the UG for years now."

The crew was silent, each face aglow in a subtle, blue light. It might have been a beautiful sight, were it not undergirded by the sheer human suffering that occurred on-board.

Along with Katarina—the soldier—and the Captain and the kid and the peace officer—himself—there was also a religious figure named Sahana perched in one dark corner of the ship's flight deck.

It was customary for a religious officer to preside over the more... delicate aspects of a diplomatic mission, from giving solace to mourning families to ensuring burial of the dead and last rites were performed in a sensible manner.

This religious priestess, Sahana, was a cleric whose practices ran toward the arcane and mystical, but she was effective, practical, and quiet, so she was a welcome member of the crew.

It did not hurt that some of her people had a distant kinship with the Xenogradians—along with a religious tie—and so it made sense for someone of her...stature to come along on this mission.

Sahana, who was an orphan of sorts—her ship had been destroyed a long time ago—said, "I sense something evil coming off that ship."

"Everything about that goddamn place is evil," said a voice from behind them.

Guerra turned to see Coulson—the ship's medic and resident hell raiser—standing in the doorway. He was unshaven and reeked of booze.

"Glad to see you could join us," the Captain said.

"We're just landing this junker," Coulson replied. "What's to see?"

Guerra unfurled to his full height and said, "We are the first corps of outsiders to be granted entry to the ARK, ever since they locked up shop. You need to take each and every aspect of this mission seriously."

Coulson smirked. "And you need to take yourself a little *less* seriously."

Guerra's eyes narrowed. "Coulson, if I have to—"

"If you have to *what*? Speak to me in *harsh tones*? Give me a formal *dressing down*? You're a bureaucrat. The only one here I report to is Katarina, and she doesn't seem bothered by my comments."

Katarina watched with detached amusement. Her eyes sparkled at the prospect of conflict.

Just then, the ship jolted as if struck by something, and Guerra's hand clenched on the back of the Captain's chair.

"It's a little hinky going in," Cap said. "We need to make a decision about how and where we're putting this puppy down."

The UG vessel was a simple unit, meant only for scouting and diplomatic expeditions. Most of the people on-board were associated with the embassy arm of the UG, so there was no grand carpet to be rolled out for them.

Especially not by Hadrian Dysart.

Dysart had inherited this...kingdom from his father, and though the ARK had always been a source of disdain by the large collection of ships that comprised the United Galaxy, recently its leader had begun a vicious crackdown on his own people to consolidate power and silence dissent.

Or so they had heard.

It was this mission—whose sole purpose was to lay the groundwork for future negotiations—that would reveal the ARK's regime for what it was.

A military dictatorship.

Looking at the ARK, Guerra said, "I don't like it. Any of it."

He stared stone-faced at the approaching target, which floated like an object suspended in gel.

"But we've come all this way," Coulson responded, the smirk never leaving his face.

"We've got to put the ship down," Captain said.

"No," Guerra said. He clenched his teeth for a moment before adding, "If we drop anchor and make unwanted contact with the ARK, they can eschew our sanctions and continue what they're doing. It will invalidate all of the work we've done—"

"And you'd rather let the people of this nation starve?" Coulson replied. Sahana, the mystic, had taken up a spot just behind his shoulder. "Let them be tortured and brainwashed? Is that worth following protocol?"

"If we don't follow protocol," Guerra responded coolly, "then we forfeit the right to intervene. That's usually when things get worse, not better."

"What do we do?" Cap asked. "We have enough fuel for this trip and the return. Anything beyond that, we're screwed. So, end this face-off so we can move ahead with our business."

Guerra clenched his teeth again. "Okay," he said. "I vote we turn back. Get re-authorization and return when we've made sufficient contact."

"Fuck that," Coulson replied. "They know we're coming. They don't answer, that's *their* fault, not ours. We go down."

Coulson glanced at Sahana, who said, "We cannot control their actions, only our own. I fear what we may find within their ship, but I fear more what will transpire if we turn our backs."

Coulson said, "Fuckin' A. We go in there and get those poor bastards out. Well, the ones we can fit, anyway."

The new guy, Sterling, said, "I could go either way."

Coulson rolled his eyes.

Katarina glanced once at Guerra and then nodded at Coulson.

The decision was made.

"Fine," Guerra said, "but I'll be documenting this in the report when we get back. I'll name each and every—"

"You go ahead and do that, G," Coulson said. "I wouldn't expect any less of you. Meanwhile, I'll be accepting all the humanitarian awards and whatnot on your behalf, if you don't mind."

They reached the exterior landing zone, and the Captain reversed the jets to slow them down.

The ARK was, like every other floating country out here in space, a grand sight. Meant to house every person lucky enough to be spirited away from the wasteland Earth had become, the ship was enormous. It beckoned the gaze of every eye that fell upon it.

Which made the thoughts of the horrors being committed inside all the more unsettling.

"Well," the Captain said, "I've had enough of the back-and-forth. We're landing this beast, and we can argue about hindsight once this is all over."

The Captain sighed and engaged his mic. He let the comm station know they were docking, even if nobody answered.

Guerra almost said something then. The words bubbled up from his chest and passed his throat before stopping in his mouth.

He was outnumbered. His entire career was based on following the rules, and yet, this was not his battle to win. These people—his *team*—had as much a say in this as he did.

This mission was as much about seeing if he could handle responsibility as it was opening up relations with a hostile, if sovereign, nation state.

Guerra knew he could put up a stink, demand they call back home to base, but that would require an investigation, going through red tape, and there was no way this group would stand for that.

Or wait for it.

They'd end up going in the ARK ship *and* resenting him, and he didn't want that, either.

"What if there's something wrong?" the new guy asked. His eyes were wide and frightened, and even though he was brand new, Guerra had been possessed of a similar thought.

Instead of giving in to his impulse to agree, though, he smiled and said, "There's nothing to worry about. We have the whole of the galaxy on our side. We're going to be safe and sound."

And that was that.

Whatever their initial thoughts and feelings, it was time to suit up.

"Let's get to it," Cap said. "I don't want to be here one second longer than necessary. This place gives me the fucking *creeps*."

2

Guerra returned to his bunk, where he prepared for the descent. He needed to gather some supplies—and his own mental well-being—before they engaged with the Dysart Administration.

The immediate goals were simple: head inside, get a lay of the land, and convince Dysart to sign a meaningless document inviting him to join the table at the UG's Security Council.

It was a show of good faith on the UG's part, but Guerra did not suspect they would actually follow through with it.

The United Galaxy was an administrative group, sound at delivering judgment on ship-borne peoples, but rarely able to actually *accomplish* anything.

They were bureaucrats, all right. Coulson had it right. They were the cogs in the machine. Rats in the maze. They did things because it made them *feel* important.

Not because they actually *were* important.

And plus, the treaty was an empty gesture. The ARK would no more be able to effect change in the Security Council than Guerra would be able to leap across the galaxy.

They just wanted to keep tabs.

And Guerra was fine with that. He could keep tabs with the best of them. He could return to the main base to report what he had seen and wash his hands of this whole matter.

Then, a voice inside him—one he knew well—interjected in his train of thought.

Nothing is going to change, it said. Everything will go badly, and you will be stuck to clean up the wreckage of this piss-poor mission.

He fought his conscience, but something kept him at arm's length from the fear welling inside him.

Meaningless diplomatic mission or not, Guerra was putting his life at risk just by *being* here.

They didn't call him *Dysart the Mad* for nothing. He was legitimately one of the more frightening entities in the galaxy, and the fact that he'd gone dark as they approached was nothing, if not terrifying.

Good thing was, he had the right kind of muscle backing him. The bad thing was, he didn't know if he had the gall to actually employ it.

Could he—if provoked—command someone like Coulson or Katarina to pull the trigger?

When he reached the door to his quarters, he slid his keycard and entered silently. Solemnly.

The auto lights flickered on, and he was startled by the appearance of a figure on his bunk.

"Sahana," he said, "How did you—"

She waved off the explanation. It was a gesture that looked practiced, like she'd done it a million times before. "Don't bother. Just know I can."

"What—what can I do for you?"

She smiled wanly. "You were outvoted back there."

Guerra busied himself with something on his desk to avoid eye contact. "No big deal," he said. "If this is the way it goes, then it's the way it goes. I can't change any of that."

"But you are worried."

"Dysart is a violent thug, and he's convinced his people he's some kind of Golden God. If we don't stop him now, there's a chance he will rule until his death, and that will result—"

"In the end of his people."

"The end of Xenograd itself," he said. "The ARK will be a floating tomb, the people of Xenograd a casualty to his grim vanity."

At this, he did make eye contact. He wanted her to know that he understood the *actual* end game of this whole dalliance.

Sahana uncrossed her legs and slid off Guerra's bunk. She was tall and slender, like all of her ancestors, and intensely striking. She was outfitted in her ship's traditional garb, a purple sari with matching body paint to accentuate her unique complexion.

She was a grand example of her people, and if he thought hard enough, Guerra might come close to naming her people's Earth country. Only historians really kept up with such gobbledygook, but he prided himself on being knowledgeable about most aspects of statecraft.

She noticed him noticing her and smiled. It wasn't an emotional gesture, but rather an intellectual one, as if she were playing a game only she knew the rules to.

"My people believed purple to be a regal color," she said, seemingly reading his thoughts. "Also, they contended that it conducts the kind of mental electricity that allows us to—"

"Commune with the God Spirit?" Guerra said.

"*Who* can read *whose* mind?" she asked, smiling.

This time, it seemed genuine.

"So," she said, "you think everyone aboard is hiding from us? Or do you suppose Dysart has already executed them all?"

"You're very casual for a mystic."

"I'm not as stuffy as the rest of my kin," she said. "I saw what fundamentalism does to a society."

Of this last fact, he had no doubt. Her homeland had been wrecked by the actions of a brutal and authoritarian religious sect. Al-Hafi, led by the gregarious and unstable Bashalahar the Barefoot, committed innumerable war crimes in the name of their strange form of religious mysticism.

A violent stand-off ensued, in which their home planet—a floating ship filled with people—was destroyed in a cataclysmic explosion.

Sahana herself was a refugee of that extended reign of terror, and she avoided the nastiness associated with the place of her raising by submitting to service in the UG.

In that way, she was overtly aligned with the other members of Guerra's crew. They were *all* misfits, in one way or another, even if they hadn't been made so by the utter destruction of their worlds.

Reflecting on all of these things in a page way, Guerra said, "I believe that is the value you bring to this mission. Your keen insight on the nature of—forgive me—cultish behavior."

Her expression revealed nothing. She said, "Which is why you didn't oppose my vote on entering the ship."

Guerra cleared his throat. "My goal *was* to follow protocol and procure helpful intelligence. Now, it's simply to keep everyone safe."

"Spoken like a true company man," she said.

"It's the truth," Guerra replied. "If any of you gets injured in the line of duty, it's on my head. I'll be expelled from my post—"

"And that's not to say your conscience won't be the worst part of it."

Guerra tried to smile, but it was a sad affair.

"You lost some people back in your home ship, did you not?"

"I—" he began, but then he shook his head. "I'd rather not talk about it."

"You don't have to," she said. "I can see the dark aura surrounding you. It makes me pause at glancing further in."

Guerra grimaced. "I'd rather you stay out of my brain, thank you very much," he said.

"Suit yourself," she replied, turning toward the exit.

After Sahana left, Guerra sat on his bunk and reflected on the people and the situations which had brought him to this moment, and he wept.

3

The staff quarters lay at the end of a long hallway on the ship's underbelly. An errant asteroid scraping the wrong side of the Arumishi would take out the whole crew, it was said, but it was more spacious than other vessels Guerra had inhabited, so he didn't mind the threat of death as much.

He was the first dressed, so he was the first to pass back through the hall leading to the elevator that would take him to the flight deck.

Katarina sat naked on her bunk, a tuft of hair on her mostly shaved head falling over one eye. She was smoking a cigar and polishing her assault rifle, which she insisted on keeping on her person at all times. The UG guidelines be damned. She didn't speak much, but her weapon was omnipresent, and she didn't hesitate to use it.

She didn't make an attempt to cover herself as Guerra passed, not that it surprised Guerra. The soldier was unencumbered by the complications of female sexuality. She'd been trained to ignore her gender at a young age, and she regarded anyone who would be distracted by such a thing as weak and ineffectual.

Coulson flipped Guerra off as he passed, and Guerra ignored it. He thought the ship's medic—who had some military training—

might have also muttered a salty epithet about Guerra's people under his breath, but he ignored that, too.

The peace officer had never worked with Coulson, but according to the personnel file, his antagonism to authority was outmatched only by his plethora of skills.

The new guy—Sterling—was searching up something on his computer and snapped the lid shut when Guerra passed by.

"Hey, um," he began, but Guerra held up one hand to cut him off.

"It's no big deal," he said, leaning through the door to the kid's private quarters. "You don't have to make small talk."

"Thanks," the young guy responded quietly.

Guerra was about to walk away when Sterling cleared his throat.

"Yes?"

"I know why everyone thinks I'm here," he said, "but that's only half the truth. My folks are rich and everything, but—"

"Listen," Guerra began. "I don't—"

"I'm good at a great many things," Sterling continued, cutting him off. "And I will carry my weight on this mission."

Guerra smiled gently. "Hey, man. We all got to start somewhere. This is just *your* beginning, you know?"

Sterling, perched on his bunk, seemed prepared to launch into a speech, but instead he exhaled and returned to his former position.

"It's just," he said, "with the war and all, these positions come at a premium, and though I didn't ask to be put here—that was all my parents—I will make every effort to do what is appropriate of someone in my position."

"I wouldn't ask anything less of you," Guerra said. "It's your job, after all. And an important one, at that. Now get set. This will get intense pretty quickly."

"Thanks," he said, and then he went back to his computer, so Guerra left him to whatever business he was conducting.

Cap was busy putting something or another back together in the ship's flight deck. The Arumishi was a good craft, but Guerra suspected it took a special kind of person to keep it running.

Hence, the Captain.

"Always fucking something," he said, chuckling to himself. "You sure you want to go through with this? I mean, the things I've heard about Dysart would straighten out your pubic hairs."

Guerra peered at the giant structure through the window with something like unease. "Whatever's going on in there has to stop. I imagine we'll take a look around, try not to ruffle any feathers—"

"Good luck with that maniac Coulson on-board," the Captain said, wiggling further under the console near his seat. "That son-of-a-bitch is liable to get you all killed."

"Coulson's all talk," Guerra replied. "He knows when to shut his mouth and listen to reason."

The Captain slid back out from under the console. "For your sake, I hope that's true."

"What do you think, Cap?"

"About what?"

"About us going in there with no indication that they want us?"

The old man smiled. "Well, it's like you said, there's atrocities going on in there and—"

"The unvarnished truth," Guerra said, cutting him off.

Cap took a moment, rubbing his hands together. "I think it's crazy to step one foot inside there," he said at last. "The UG is a—how can I say it?—an organization of *conflict resolution*. This place"—he pointed out the window—"needs to have somebody set fire to it, like it was covered in spiders, and never look back."

"You really think so?"

"I'm old, kid," he replied. "I've seen some horrible things in my time. I was a smuggler of one sort or another in my day, and back then, there was no United Galaxy to coerce nations into playing nice."

"I've heard some things about the way it used to be."

"Yeah, it wasn't pretty. But the UG hasn't been forced to deal with a country that doesn't want to play ball, and the ARK doesn't want to play ball. You know why we all live up here instead of down here in the first place, don't you?"

"Of course I do."

It had been hundreds and hundreds of years since humans had inhabited their home planet, and though the stories about it varied, one thing was made clear: it was an uninhabitable mess down there.

"Well, then," the old man said sardonically, "you have a good idea of what I think is happening. Us pussyfooting into their home isn't going to solve anything. You want my take, we need to escort all the innocents out and forget this place ever fucking existed."

"You don't honestly believe that, do you? As a member of the UG?"

"Son, you've got a healthy respect for the rules, and so do I, when I think they'll work."

"And you don't think they'll work here?"

The old man smiled sadly. "You'll see. Just give it time."

4

They were standing on the edge of the ship's back lift when Coulson asked his first annoying question.

"So, what happens if we kick in the door and find some shit we are not prepared to deal with?"

Guerra was about to answer when Katarina raised her assault rifle. She didn't say anything to clarify, but the meaning was taken.

"I guess that makes sense," Coulson replied, "but seriously, what if Billie Holiday Badass over there can't take all the jackbooted thugs down?"

Katarina shrugged and lowered her weapon.

"I don't know, Coulson," Guerra said.

Sahana sighed.

"We all die," she said simply.

"That's fucking comforting," Coulson replied. "Any particular reason you think that? You look into your crystal ball before we stepped down here?"

She glanced unsteadily at the ship rising into blackness in front of them. "I can sense it," she said. "The energy coming from inside...it's not good."

"Oh, great," Coulson replied. "So the bureaucrat was right. To avoid getting our nuts lopped off, maybe we do head back inside and scurry to the home base."

Guerra gripped his force gun a little tighter. He could feel his jaw getting sore from clenching his teeth, but he refused to give Coulson the satisfaction of losing his cool.

"We were selected," he said. "This is our *duty*. I didn't want to land, but now that we're here, we have a job to do, and by Saint Oliver and Adrian of Nicomedia, we are going to do it to the best of our ability. Now, if you want to head back upstairs to the flight deck—"

The Captain interrupted. "I'm not going anywhere, so if you run into trouble, just high-tail it back here, and I'll lift us off to safety. No problem."

"That's comforting," Coulson said, not without a smirk. "I guess he means just outrun the slowest person, am I right?"

There was no answer from the group.

A moment later, the cargo deck clicked and began to open, lowering them toward the ARK's formal entrance.

But Coulson was still worrying his old saw. His glowering smile widened. "How's your forty yard dash, Guerra?"

But Guerra had already turned his attention away from the fly in his ointment and toward the monstrosity of a ship in front of them.

The ARK—which housed the people of Xenograd. Or, formerly of Xenograd.

It was almost impossible to believe an entire country could fit inside a single floating craft, but here they were.

There were hundreds of ships like this one in the solar system, but this one—it was special.

Majesty and horror, all at a single clip. The best and worst of human existence. A testament to the fact that anything could be accomplished—any problem could be vanquished—if enough human misery was thrown at it.

Of all the countries that remained—really, the ones that survived the scramble to leave Earth—Xenograd was the worst of the best.

Or at least the worst of what remained.

True, some countries didn't make it, but many—the industrialized ones, anyway—did.

Survival of the fittest.

Well—the richest, anyway.

It was an unsettling truth, but a truth nonetheless, that the countries incapable of footing their own evacuation received no quarter from the other countries.

Guerra's ancestors—everyone's ancestors—bore witness to a passive extermination of half the human population, probably more. It could have been as high as seventy-five or eighty percent, but those kinds of records were closely kept, and most people were just happy to be alive, given what Earth itself looked like these days.

And there was no rhyme or reason to it. No moralistic line to draw from the actions of a people to their ultimate survival.

It was just money.

Rich, corrupt banana republics and iron-fisted dictatorships pulled the same kind of inside straight, while smaller, more religiously upright countries died by the fire their prophecies commanded would only consume the wicked.

It wasn't a judgment handed down by an omnipotent being.

It was a *tribulation*.

A cause of great suffering given to the righteous and the iniquitous equally. Humanity was to endure this, at the risk of total extinction, and what gift did they have to look forward to?

Nothing.

That was God's great promise.

Empty, black fucking space, and nothing more.

Guerra himself wasn't a religious man—at least not currently—but he had been raised in the Hispanic form of the Roman Catholic tradition by a fundamentalist father, so he understood the joyous anxiety associated with the end of the world.

Still, he thought it odd that God had forsaken so many, while allowing the people of the ARK (and other likely terrorist states) to persist. To *thrive*, even.

It gave Guerra a vaguely eerie sensation to contemplate it, so he decided to pack away his feelings.

For now.

Sterling asked, "If this guy is so bad, why did the UG allow him to become such a tyrant before stepping in?"

"Money," Coulson said. "It's always about fucking money."

Guerra rolled his eyes and readied himself to explain everything, but the Captain, in his infinite wisdom, decided to step in via the installed headsets in their suits. "Dysart is a third-rate dictator, but he's a first-rate dipshit," he said. "He helped create a political vacuum, and then his fat, mustachioed ass filled the vacuum. He thought he could manipulate people into silence and servitude, but human nature doesn't quite work like that, I'm afraid."

"Thanks, Cap," Guerra said. "The only thing I'll add is that this guy uses torture and murder to maintain order. Roving death squads, committing extrajudicial killings against dissidents, as his juries and executioners."

"Wow," Sterling replied.

"It's bad," Guerra said. "And the sooner we get the hell out of this place, the better I think we will all feel."

GUERRA LED the group to the ship's main entrance for commerce and foreign policy. It was a simple bay festooned with bright colors and welcoming posters.

However, the bay itself was closed and dark, the motion sensor and opening mechanisms completely nonfunctioning.

"Well, this is fucked," Coulson said.

"It's like somebody just turned out the lights," the Captain said into their headphones.

"How do we get in?" Sterling asked.

The ARK was outfitted with hundreds of ship bays, and so it wouldn't be impossible to find another dock—eventually.

But it was a stalling tactic. The ship was obviously intact and working just fine, in other regards.

"We'll have to use the torch," Guerra said. "Katarina?"

The soldier nodded and unslung a giant blowtorch from her pack. Katarina was outfitted with a whole bevy of tools, in part because she was accustomed to each and every one of them.

She had been a mercenary for many years before landing in the employ of the United Galaxy. A lifelong fighter, Katarina had spent her youth getting paid to help systematically overthrow unstable or autocratic regimes.

For a time, she became one of the most wanted people in all the galaxy, but then something happened, and she turned herself into the UG, expecting—Guerra was sure—to spend the remainder of her life in a space station version of the Hague.

Eventually, a deal was struck, and she became what she had always been. Only, this time, she was fighting for the good guys. At least that what it seemed she chose to believe.

There was also the rumor about her parents, but no one dared bring that up in her presence.

As Katarina worked, Guerra made contact with his superiors back at the UG. "Guerra here. They didn't roll out the red carpet, so we are forcing our way inside."

A laconic, slightly robotic voice responded. "Protocol indicates—"

"Yeah, I know," he replied. "I was outvoted. Simple as that. But we are taking a simple look-see inside, and then we'll report back with findings before heading back to the main ship."

"Very well. It should be noted that you not make any unwarranted movements without express consent."

"Copy that."

"This is a delicate diplomatic endeavor, and an mistake will—"

The next words cut out, and when Guerra asked the voice to repeat for clarification, he got nothing in return.

Just static.

5

"Seems like the signal is suffering major interference," the Captain said from back in the ship. "I'll go work on the audio racks and see what I can do. In the meantime, you keep your wits about you. I can't save you if I can't hear you, and I don't want to get stranded out here. Place gives me the creeps, officially speaking."

"Of course," Guerra replied, but he felt somewhat unsettled himself. There was something about this place—even beyond its closely guarded reputation—that made him uneasy.

Meanwhile, the rest of the crew had spread out to lock down the perimeter. Also—to avoid speaking with one another. They weren't as close as some crews, and this mission was the UG equivalent of gruntwork, anyway, so they just had to stick together until they returned to the Arumishi.

Then, they could go their separate ways.

So to speak.

Guerra checked each person's location. On the far edge of the ship, Sahana was meditating, sitting cross-legged with her suit back facing the rest of the group.

Coulson, for whatever reason, was punching a wall. His mic was off, but Guerra could see him screaming angrily inside his mask.

And Sterling—where *was* Sterling?

He popped his mic and called for the newbie. Getting nothing in return but more signal interference, he tied off and headed for the far edge of the ship, to the darkest corner of this little staging area.

"Sterling?"

Guerra steeled himself for a bad outcome. It wasn't uncommon for greenhorns to get entangled in something bad and end up floating off into the darkness, never to be seen again.

Sterling didn't seem like the type, though.

He engaged his internal mic and held in a breath as he spoke, his chest tight and his throat no better. "Sterling? You copy?"

Someone responded, but it was a mess of distortion and broken syllables, so he couldn't even determine the voice's gender, let alone the particulars. It could have been Coulson or the Captain or Katarina, for that matter.

Well, probably not Katarina.

The panic crept out of its hiding hole, like a spider emerging from the crack in a wall, and so Guerra thumbed the safety on his blast gun and flicked the charge button. The gun hummed in his hands. At full capacity, a single discharge from the weapon could tear a full-grown man into pieces.

He rested his finger on the trigger guard.

"Sterling?" he said, approaching the darkest corner of the ship's outer hull. Ships almost definitely did not land out here. They entered the docking bay and proceeded from there. The fact that the crew was out here already sent a bad message. Guerra was not Sahana and thus did not believe in karma, but something about this gave him a bad feeling.

He had seen atrocities before. Earthlings once had sidestepped mutually-assured destruction once, in an effort to leave their home planet.

That didn't mean humanity had overcome the propensities which had once landed them at nuclear midnight. Human beings were still a hateful, petulant, self-involved race, with as many bigotries as they once had.

Maybe more.

Now that each country was its own ship—and, thus, its own civilization—the homogeny of race and religion had isolated entire cultures, and those cultures had grown suspect of the other ships.

Guerra hated it, but that was just the way it was.

Then, just as he was about to call for the young guy again, a figure moved in the shadows. Guerra's finger flexed, and he almost fired but managed to hold back when he saw who it was.

Sterling appeared out of nowhere, smiling and waving. "Just decided to see what was on the other side," he said.

Huh, Guerra thought. Seemed unlikely, but what the hell did he know? He was once an ambitious young buck in the system. Maybe Sterling thought he could find his *own* way in.

"Well," he said, "don't wander off by yourself again. I know you're new and this feels like a vacation from your former post, but I can guarantee some bad things have happened inside this ship. So stay close and stay alert. There will come a time when we will need you."

"Somehow I doubt that."

Guerra stopped. "Listen," he said. "You're a rich kid. Everybody knows, so yeah, Katarina probably won't end up clapping you on the back and calling you *comrade*, but you have a distinct function here. Right?"

"Right."

"You know plenty about the Dysart regime, and you have memorized the internal layout of this ship. You know we need that, right?"

"Right."

"Okay, so you are a necessity on this trip, just as much as Cap or Sahana, and I need you to behave like it. Take control of your destiny."

"Got it."

"Good."

When they returned to the ship's outer entrance, Katarina had sawed through the latch keeping them out.

"It's time," Coulson said. His voice was calm and devoid of its usual raspy contempt. "You ready?"

Guerra nodded.

Katarina then placed the fingers of her suit under the gigantic door and pulled. The rest of the crew joined in, and soon they had lifted it high enough to sneak under.

Cap's voice commanded their headset radios. "I'm going to do some routine maintenance on the ship. You need anything, just holler."

"Ten-four," Guerra said, and then they all headed to an inner chamber, where they could disrobe.

The bulky space suits were no longer needed, but they would keep their helmets on for the sake of communication and environmental protection. The helmets themselves were outfitted with complex air filters that scrubbed airborne pathogens from their midst.

And the UG outfits—with the official insignia—gave them some diplomatic protection, if they got into trouble.

"It's awfully...empty down here," Sterling said, looking around.

Coulson replied, "This is the old *anti-welcome*. They want us to fight for every inch."

"Yes," Sterling said, "but there should be security officers or logistics personnel to greet us, even if they don't want us here. That's just the way it is."

"Hold your opinions," Guerra replied. "Reserve judgment until we've made definitive contact with Dysart or his representatives. Then, you can freak out all you want."

"I'm already there," Sterling said nervously.

Once they had reached the main internal chamber, where recycled oxygen was pumped in to provide some semblance of normalcy, they stripped down to their official UG uniforms and refitted their weapon holsters.

An unexpected voice echoed in the small room.

"Weapons off and put away, safeties on."

Guerra and the rest of the group turned to find Katarina staring them down. She gave no indication that she would repeat herself, and no one dared spoil the moment by acknowledging her contribution.

Guerra merely nodded, and the group followed suit. Katarina didn't speak often, but when she did, it was for cause.

Guerra used the comms box in the corner of the room to contact the ship's main tower.

"Tower, this is KG-237, representative of the UG Alliance, here to request entry and escort. We have a scheduled meeting with the Dear Leader."

"The fuck?" Coulson said.

Guerra released the comms button. "It's a formal title, the one he made up for himself. I don't call him that, we don't make it past this room. Simple as that."

"Don't expect me to call the son-of-a-bitch that," Coulson replied. "I'd rather put a bullet in my brain."

"You worry about your lane," Guerra said, "and I'll worry about mine."

Guerra returned to his opening entreaty. "Repeat, this is KG-237, officer with the UG Alliance, requesting entry and escort. Do you copy?"

No response. Just silence on the other end.

Guerra released the button again. He was perplexed.

"They can't believe we're just going to go away," Guerra said. "A whole country cannot play possum and expect to get away with it."

Sahana positioned herself next to the door and placed both hands on it. She closed her eyes and hummed a soft, sweet melody to herself.

When she was done, she opened her eyes, which had faded from a dark black to a piercing yellow color.

There was worry in them.

"I do not sense any positive energy on the other side of this door," she said. "We will proceed from darkness to darkness, I fear."

"Well, Jesus Christ, thanks for the update," Coulson said. "Let me deal with this."

Coulson strode over to the comms box, one hand reaching into his belt for a tool of some kind, but as he did, a green light above the door flashed twice.

The door beeped and opened, providing a view of the world's vast and unnerving interior.

"Well—I'll be," Coulson said, replacing his screwdriver. "I'm even better at this than I thought."

There was no weight to his statement, however. His voice sounded as thin as Sterling's had back on the ship's bay.

Sterling filled the conversational void by saying, "We are almost dead center in the middle of this ship. Beyond this door is one of the main social areas of Xenograd."

"Social areas?" Guerra asked.

"Think of it like a mall food court," he said. "If anybody knows what one of those is. Anyway, it's a giant space, full of shopping districts and upscale homes. The original architects of this ship meant to convey the perception that this place was a free and open society."

"Well," Coulson said, "it's good to know the prison won't be the first thing we'll see."

"Actually," Sterling responded, "the prison can be found—"

"*Never. Mind*," Coulson said. "Let's get this dog and pony show started. Anybody opposed to that?"

No one said anything, so Guerra took up the lead and headed through the door into the world of the ARK proper.

6

What he and the others saw was...astounding. He had to take stock of his emotions and physical appearance, just to ensure he wasn't staring gape-mouthed at the scene in front of him.

"*Dios mio*," he said, glancing from place to place.

"Is this for real?" Sterling asked.

"'Fraid so," Coulson responded.

What stood before them, highlighted in every possible way by their surroundings, was...nothing.

"It's like somebody flipped off the lights and went home," Sterling said. "I've never seen anything like it."

There were *some* lights on—and some flickered inconsequentially—but for the most part, this whole floor of the ship was bathed in eerie darkness.

"Is this intentional?" Guerra asked. "Is this a play?"

Coulson flicked on the light attached to his head and took a few tentative steps forward. There was trash and filth and a little blood on the ground nearby.

"I don't think so," Coulson said. "It looks like something extraordinarily fucked up went down in here."

Just then, as if prompted, a low, guttural yowl filled the expanse of the court. It sounded like thunder run through a fried guitar amp, and it caught everyone, save for Katarina, off-guard.

It was ridiculous. Utterly and wholly ridiculous. Like a prank a brother might play on a fearful younger sibling.

But it wasn't.

This was dead serious, something that might mean the difference between a few thousand dead and a few *million* dead.

And though Guerra didn't know what this thing was, he felt his whole body grow stiff with the realization that they were *in it*, that the possibility of turning back was quickly fading.

Sterling was the first to speak. "We should go," he said. "Whatever that was, we should head back to the ship, and—we should really, really go."

But after a few moments, the sound subsided, and they were left again with silence. Silence—and darkness.

The neon sign above a burger joint named Freddy's Fries blinked itself into existence, the pink hum of the light giving them some—but not much—visibility.

Coulson said, "The power grid here is fucked. I think it might have been electrical."

"It didn't sound electrical," Sterling commented, "and I don't want to lose my head because you mistook—"

Coulson turned on the young guy, grabbed him by the throat. He backed him against the wall and said, "Mistook *what*? You think we somehow landed in the midst of a horror movie?"

"I—I don't know," Sterling said. "That's what I'm afraid of."

Coulson peered into the kid's frightened eyes for a few more seconds and then seemed to realize that he wasn't worth it.

"Give me a break," he said. "If it isn't something to do with the power grid, it's probably the dying wail of one of the poor sons-of-bitches that lives here."

Guerra's throat clicked as he swallowed. "Calm down, Coulson. This isn't any time to get riled up."

"Tell that to the boy wonder over there," Coulson replied. "He's the one thinks we've wandered into *The Twilight Zone*."

Sterling gave him a curious look. "What's that?"

Coulson shrugged.

Sterling huffed for a few seconds, then said, "Let's go."

He turned away, and Guerra hoped nobody else heard the way the tears seemed to catch in the kid's throat.

He really isn't ready for this, Guerra thought.

But this trip was one hell of a way to toughen him up. If the folks were looking for a way to make sure he was ready to handle the inheritance, this was an extreme way of doing it.

"So," Guerra said, "we want to make the trek in? Or do we go back to our ship and report everything?"

Coulson's laugh was mocking. "Report what? We haven't seen anything."

"There's plenty we won't want to see," Sahana said. "And I fear to know what lies in the darkness."

Coulson took a few definitive steps forward. "Only one way to find out."

Everyone turned back to the path before them to find Katarina standing near a door leading into the main, high-ceilinged hall.

And she had her gun out—the only assault weapon allowed on this mission.

The safety was off.

Coulson looked at Guerra, who shrugged. "Hey," he said, "we violated protocol when we sawed open the hatch back there. Everything from here on in is free poker."

"Well, then," Coulson replied. "Let's go all-in."

7

They walked for a little while in the width and breadth of the giant plaza, and only occasionally did anyone comment on how eerie it was that the place was stone cold empty.

Mostly, though, they just filed along in silence, the sound of their boots or the occasional whistling filling the air.

Finally, Guerra had to say something.

"It doesn't make any sense," Guerra said. "I've been in war-torn ships. I've seen ethnic cleansing. And this isn't it. This likes like everyone just sort of...went away."

"Maybe they did," Sahana said.

He was reminded again of the idea of tribulation. Of Revelation, God's signal that the world was ending.

"How's that?" Coulson responded.

"In my homeland, people were known to disappear all the time. The disappearances were always paired with news stories about strangers snatching little children, but everyone knew better."

"Well, if it wasn't a kiddie fiddler," Coulson asked, "who or what could it have been, then? Mass delusion?"

"Rapture," she replied without looking at any of them.

Coulson smirked. "Like I said, 'mass delusion.'

"Don't," Guerra said, and then he stopped.

In that moment, Katarina was out front with her weapon in tow.

"Stand down, Kat," Guerra said. "It's the light."

Guerra pointed to a blinking light coming from one of the shops to their right. This area seemed to be a little more well-lit than the rest of the promenade, but the last few buildings had been completely without power.

But it was true. Inside an old candy shop lay a small box made of a glassy material, blinking as though someone had recorded a missing message.

"It's a Vault-o-Phone," Sterling said, half-stammering.

"A *what*?" Coulson asked. His voice was full of a new brand of contempt. He sounded like he had been served shards of glass for dinner.

"A VO Phone," Sterling replied. "It's an audio recording someone makes, usually to commemorate some kind of special occurrence—a birthday or a historical event. I imagine this one probably has something else entirely on it, though."

Sterling went after it, and the rest of them filed in afterward.

On the front of the item was the title FOUNDER'S DAY, and the name Daphne Farentino blinked just below it.

"Well," Guerra said, "let's see what Daphne has to say."

"Maybe she's telling everyone where to hide for our surprise party," Coulson said. "Part of me doesn't want to ruin it."

Guerra gave him an *eat shit* look, just as Sterling pressed the small PLAY button. The hiss of audio was followed by a bright and cheerful female voice.

IT IS A GLORIOUS DAY, *indeed! The Founder—Dysart, Dysart—has blessed us with eternity, and we take this time, this day, to celebrate HIM. May God bless the ceremony and all the attendees, and may the ARK see the end of the galaxy.*

Oh, and anyone wishing to attend said ceremony should travel swiftly to the Founder's Garden, where the festivities will begin approximately at sundown. Or whenever Dear Leader chooses to dim the ship's lights. Hope to see you there! I will be the woman in the red hat.

"Founder's Day?"

Sterling shrugged. "It appears Dysart turned himself into a near-religious figure."

"Wait a second," Coulson replied. "I thought you were the expert on this whole situation. What the fuck did we bring you along for, if not this?"

"I know the layout of the ship and some history. This place is like an intellectual black hole. Nothing gets in or out without Dysart knowing about it. That's why we cannot know exactly what happened here."

"Well," Guerra said, "hopefully, there are more of these along the path, because I, for one, need to know more context about this situation before turning and heading back to the ship."

Sahana said, "Or maybe heading back to the ship is the ultimate display of knowledge, since every step forward takes us closer to the unknown."

Coulson smiled. "I thought you would like that freaky hoodoo shit. Maybe Dysart can be your new god."

"I value the unknown," Sahana replied, "but I value my life even more."

Guerra nodded but kept going. He returned to the main path, his thoughts swirling like a terrible storm in his mind.

"Still," he said, "we can't turn around now. If things get hairy, we can beat a hasty retreat, but for now, let's see where this takes us. If there are people in danger, we need to do what we can to help get them out of this place."

Coulson looked around, noting the darkness. "*If* there are any people left," he said. "And I'm not so sure there are."

Guerra paid attention to their surroundings as they hiked

through this giant, open market of a location. Stores lined the walkway, but they all appeared to be broken-down versions of themselves.

Each building was destroyed or ransacked, but the patina of dust on everything also indicated maybe it wasn't *new*, either.

One store featured a sign boasting **WE HAVE FOOD!**, while another with busted out windows advertised **MODS FOR CHEAP**.

"The hell are mods?" Coulson asked.

Sterling ventured off the beaten path and clicked the button on his head-mounted light. When he peered into the depths of the store, all that was revealed—at least in Guerra's eyes—was junk. Ripped boxes and shards of glass, all surrounding cheap-o store displays with happy-looking and genetically-modified customers.

"Modifications," Sterling said. "Looks like they were toying with genetic enhancements."

Guerra had heard of better living through chemistry, but no such nonsense as this. Those people inside—the store displays—looked not like human beings but like *monsters*. Could this be one of the reasons the ship was so empty? Had people accidentally overdosed on some madman's elixir?

"Sounds like horseshit to me," Coulson responded. "I've been to places where people thought they had some form of this nailed down. Didn't call it *modding* or whatever, but they were neck-deep in the stuff. People drinking crazy potions and shooting themselves up with who knows what, all because they thought they could reverse the ravages of time."

"Or bad biological make-up," Sterling said. He was sounding more confident than he had in the ship. "When you think about it, Dysart was one of those Hitler types."

Coulson rolled his eyes. "Can't we go to at least one galactic dystopia without *Hitler* being brought up?"

"It's true, though," Sterling continued, not getting Coulson's joke. "Dysart purportedly was obsessed with the purity and the virility of his people. It would make sense for him to want them to improve themselves in any way possible."

"Either way," Coulson responded, "it doesn't work. When will people learn: you can't change the central aspects of living? Death, disease, sickness, decay. These things are going to happen, and—"

"Shhhh."

Everyone turned to Katarina, who had edged further down the promenade. She had her assault rifle out and at the ready. Guerra and the rest of them went instantly silent and held their breath.

Listening. Eyes darting helplessly into the darkness.

Katarina uttered four words that sent shivers through Guerra.

"We are not alone."

And then the lights came on.

All of them.

8

It was like somebody had flipped on a giant light switch. The entirety of the ARK was flooded with dull, fluorescent illumination. What had been a dark cavern of failed electronics and wires was now a flickering oasis in the midst of the stars.

However, revealing all of the nooks and crannies of the ARK ship did nothing to ease Guerra's anxiety about this particular mission.

If there was no one left to save—or, in the case of Dysart, no one left to use as a bargaining chip—then what were Guerra and the rest of them worth?

Nothing.

Less than nothing.

If Dysart decided to spare them at all, they probably wouldn't leave the ARK without enduring at least *some* torture.

Guerra sighed, looked around.

Someone had destroyed the food court and moved on to some other area in Xenograd to destroy.

However, with the light came a new understanding of the (for lack of a better word) *land* they had come to investigate.

"Look at all the propaganda," Guerra said.

The walls were plastered with life-sized posters depicting Xenograd's leader in a stance of dominance.

Dysart, standing guard over the ship, dressed in frilly, faux-European garb, a steely gaze focused on the viewer.

IF YOU ARE COMMITTED TO DYSART, the poster read, **IT IS YOUR DUTY TO IDENTIFY OUTSIDERS.**

In another poster, a woman, vaguely brown-skinned, staring menacingly at the viewer.

PROTECT THE PURITY OF XENOGRAD, it read. **SEE AN OUTSIDER, SAY SOMETHING NOW.**

And there were dozens and dozens of these posters lining the walls and windows, tacked up as if done in a hurry.

Like the strands of power were quickly untethering.

"Looks like *1984* took a shit on the walls, doesn't it?"

"It's terrible," Guerra replied, "*and* plentiful."

"I don't get it," Coulson said. "What's with this Xenograd bullshit? I thought this was the ARK?"

Sterling said, "ARK's the ship, and Xenograd is the city within. Kind of like a soccer field being named something different than the stadium itself."

"Well, whoop-de-fucking do," Coulson replied.

"You *asked*," Sterling said.

Sterling, stepping away from the group, walked over to one of the posters and studied it closely.

"It's interesting," he said. "This doesn't look like your typical, run-of-the-mill propaganda."

"It doesn't?" Guerra asked.

Sterling shook his head. "If I had to guess, this was the result of a concerted effort to overthrow Dysart," he said. "This message is about reassurance. I'm sure we'll find some other material villainizing the opposition, or resistance, which is what they probably preferred to be called."

"How do you know all this?" Coulson asked.

Sterling turned back to them, his face a sad picture of familial angst. "My father was one hell of a propagandist himself."

"Let's keep moving," Katarina said. "I feel the walls closing in."

"So do I," Sahana replied. "And something horrid awaits us at the end of this walk."

Guerra took one last look at the receding pin prick of an exit door back the way they had come, and he sighed.

"Sterling, how far away is the UG embassy?"

The new guy seemed to contemplate that. "Not far," he said. "If memory serves, we can reach it by cutting across the Memorial Garden at the far end of this road."

"Good," Coulson said. "More walking."

"You can complain," Guerra said, "or you can come with us."

"Oh, I can do both," Coulson replied. "I'm pretty good at multi-tasking."

Each store's name was either a direct or indirect rip-off of the Dysart name, and those storefronts displaying his likeness had been destroyed.

"It's amazing that someone can get to be so powerful, so influential," Coulson said, shaking his head. "I always thought I'd be a good cult leader, but Christ, it seems like a lot of work."

Sterling cleared his throat. "Dysart began his career as a general and then transitioned into the political world. He often wore his military garb but wrapped his head in a traditional scarf to denote his religious conviction."

Coulson pointed to one of the wall length posters above them—the thing had to be a hundred feet tall, if not more—and said, "This guy managed to convince people he was some kind of religious warrior?"

Sterling shrugged.

Sahana filled in the conversation. "When people need to believe —when they feel they have no choice *but* to believe—it is remarkable the inconsistencies they will ignore in favor of hope. It happens everywhere."

"I guess so," Coulson said dubiously.

"Even with us," Sahana said. "We have ignored all signs of danger in favor of the idea that we can make a difference."

"What else you got?" Coulson asked.

Sterling said, "Well, after he unified the church, the military, and the government, he assassinated all the leaders of the opposing parties and finished consolidating power. And then the ship went dark. Nothing after that."

"How do you know so much about this jagoff?"

"Because it is my job to know, just as it is your job to silence people with the tools of your trade."

"Well, isn't that fucking enlightening?"

"It's the truth," Sterling shot back.

Guerra intervened. "That's enough, both of you. Sterling, lead us to the garden shortcut, and Coulson—"

"Yeah, boss."

"Shut the fuck up."

"Ten-four."

9

Guerra's mic beeped, and the Captain rang in. "How's everything looking in there?"

"Good," Guerra replied, deciding not to mention the haunted house sounds coming from in the darkness, "but your signal is a bit fuzzy. How's the transmitter looking outside?"

"You...fine...me," came the reply. "Just...me know...can do."

Shit, Guerra thought.

"Something wrong?" Sahana asked.

"Comm system's a little finicky," he replied. "Should be fine overall, though. Must be in a bad location."

Coulson said, "These high-frequency numbers should be able to transmit from anywhere inside this ship, especially if the ARK systems are still functioning. It's not ideal, but we should be able to hijack their signal."

"Once we can find someone—anyone—maybe we'll do that," Guerra said. "Until then, perhaps we should stay radio silent."

Coulson smirked. "You're the one gabbing with Cap."

As they walked along, paying attention to the posters and broken-down department stores, Sahana whistled.

"In my home ship," Sahana said, "it was a plague that wiped out my people. Just came and took them away like a thief in the night."

Everyone just kept walking and looking around. Now that everything was illuminated, they could make their way quickly down the main thoroughfare, even if it was unclear *just* who had flipped the switch for them.

"Wait a sec," Sterling said, "I thought it was a civil war. Two religious factions duking it out over an area where some stone or some other such thing was being held."

Sahana smiled, but there was no mirth in it. "That's partly true," she said, "but death reared its ugly head first. This happened during the summit meant to quell the anger between—as you mentioned—the religious sects. Even though war was on the horizon, the elders of both factions agreed to meet in a central location."

"And that's how the war started?" Coulson asked.

Sahana's patience was evident, to Guerra, in how she laughed off the medic's presumption and impatience.

"I wish it were so," she replied. "It would make things so much easier, in retrospect, to know that human nature intervened to snatch war from the jaws of peace. Alas, it has to do with a human, but not humanity."

"Well, get to it, lady," Coulson replied, mostly under his breath. He was squinting at something far off in the distance.

His hackles were up. Guerra assumed *all* of theirs were, but this was a distraction—though not a pleasant one—from the questions related to what had happened here.

"We had all gathered to watch these two men, these two priests, shake hands and declare a peace. But that was not what happened. Just as the two bent figures made their way to the center of the city, a bearded man, far along in years, appeared in the town square."

"What do you mean 'appeared?'" Sterling asked.

"I mean, he was old and wisened, but unknown to my family. It was as if he were a stowaway who had waited until this moment to intervene. And, to this day, I still cannot, for the life of me, remember the contours of his face. In its place, there is a blank space."

"And you say this stranger interrupted their peace meeting? Did he give any particular reason why?"

Sterling had ignored his duty and was paying close attention to Sahana's story. He had his gun in hand but was not peering into the distance of the hallway the way the others were.

"He reared up in between the two men and said something in a foreign tongue, just before blood erupted from his nose, mouth, and eyes."

"His eyes?" Coulson asked.

"It is so strange. I can remember the blood, pouring in gouts from his face, and I can remember the twinkle in his eyes, the smile, but not the particulars of his expression. It's as though his features have been erased from memory."

"Sounds like a fucking blessing, if you ask me."

"My parents escaped the ship, along with a few hundred other refugees, just before the entire structure ignited and burst into flames. We were one of the last groups to make it out before —everything."

"Jesus."

That was Coulson.

"It sounds crazy to say, but I have spent much of my life looking for that man."

Coulson was confused. "But I thought you said—"

"Even though I know he is dead, I search for him. For his blank, bleeding face."

"You may not find him," Sterling said, "but hopefully you will find some amount of peace."

Her face turned bitter, and it was obvious she was no longer telling a story but unburdening her soul. "I do not know my people. I have never met another person like me. As far as I know, I'm the last of my kind."

Coulson said, "Aw, that's too cynical. You never know. They could be out there, fucking like beasts in an effort to repopulate—"

"Someone else's ship?" she said, her smile a dark thing on her face. "You and I both know refugees are housed like animals wherever they are. That is the reason I took up this...profession."

"Well, I'm going to put down a thousand bucks you meet one someday."

"I cannot sense their presence anywhere, just as I sense nothing but death and emptiness on this ship."

"Judging by the sound of whatever was on this floor sometime back," Coulson said, "I can tell you with certainty it's not empty. In fact, I—"

"Everybody stop," Sterling said, and everybody did.

They had reached the end of one road, where it forked into two separate lanes, and neither was distinguishable from the other.

"Unless I'm wrong," Sterling said, "the park is right down...there."

He pointed to his left. It was by far the more well-lit of the two paths, and though he was ignorant of the ship's layout, Guerra was damn glad to be going somewhere illuminated.

"All we have to do is...walk...this...way."

Guerra shined his flashlight on the ground at their feet.

Picket signs of one sort or another littered the ground, either tossed in the street or propped against the park's walls.

"Is that blood?" Sterling asked. "On the picket signs, I mean. Is that actual blood?"

Guerra checked and then cleared his throat. "Fraid so, Sterling," he said. "Looks like this was one uprising that did not result in revolution."

"More like a bloodbath," Coulson countered.

"But, then, where are the jack-booted thugs?" Sterling replied. "Seems like the police state would be in full view by now."

A great many of the signs were upside down but legible nonetheless. Some contained simple protest slogans—**NO MORE MODDING!** and **DYSART=DEATH!**—while others seemed to explain in painstaking detail the ARK's problems.

Guerra focused his attention on one that seemed to hit him in the chest.

HUMAN BLOOD IS NOT MUD. PEOPLE CANNOT BE UNTOUCHABLE.

"Look at all these signs," Sterling said. "There must be *thousands* of them here. Just kind of...abandoned."

"Maybe they'll lead us to someone who can help us out, answer a few questions," Coulson said.

Katarina did not speak, but she grunted loud enough for the rest of them to hear it.

Then, without context or preamble, she said, "These people are all dead."

10

They followed the trail of bloodied and torn protest signs, until they reached the park's gated entrance, which had been chained shut.

"Huh," Sterling said.

"Another way around?" Guerra asked.

"Yeah, but this is the most direct path," Sterling recounted.

Coulson shrugged. "Then it's over the fence we go, I guess."

"Bad idea," Sahana said.

Guerra joined Coulson by a bent portion of the fence.

"Yeah, well, I'm all out of good ideas," Guerra responded.

They helped one another over and entered the lush and elaborate garden area. The oxygen seemed cleaner here, even if the plant life itself appeared to have been mismanaged for some time.

"I bet this was beautiful at some point," Sterling said.

Long ago, when he was a little boy, Guerra was given a picture book of famous places from back home on Earth, and one of the pictorials featured the Jardin du Luxembourg, from a place called Paris. It was a verdant, lush, manicured landscape, and the pictures had featured dozens of tourists and locals basking in the illustrative beauty of the place.

His father abhorred the temptations of the flesh—even natural beauty—but he allowed his son this one indulgence, perhaps as a way of trying to connect with the homeland in his own way, and this place reminded him of that.

This garden, a monument to the Monster of Xenograd, was probably loosely based on the Jardin du Luxembourg, but no matter how many flowers they planted and how many sculptures littered the walkways, it would always be tainted by The ARK's mad ruler.

They passed the ticket booth and came to a stop in front of a giant statue of none other than Dysart.

It was a massive thing, almost painful to look at in its garishness and vainglory.

In one hand, Xenograd's leader was holding a giant sword. The other wasn't readily visible, but he was holding it out palm up, like there was a handful of beans in it.

"What's in his left hand?" Guerra asked.

Sterling stared up at it, studied it for a moment. "If I had to guess, I'd say it was something to do with the mod stations. In the statue, he is reminding them of his strength *and* his generosity."

Coulson scoffed. "As if they could fucking forget about this nitwit. There are pictures of him on every street corner."

"Which is good when things are going well," Guerra said, "but when things are bad—"

"People start rioting like *mother*fuckers," Coulson finished. "Yeah, I get it."

At the base of the statue, where the engraving would normally extol Herr Leader's multitudinous virtues, there was instead a stark bit of graffiti.

JUSTICE TO BEATRIX.

"Who the fuck is Beatrix?"

Guerra shook his head. "Yet another mystery to uncoil here in the black hole of this ship. Sterling?"

The kid examined the graffiti for a moment and then shook his head. "There's nothing in my database about her."

They moved past the statute and wandered, guns in tow, down the garden's main path.

"You know, this is weird to say," Coulson said, breaking the silence, "but this is an enchanting little distraction."

"Shut up," Guerra replied. "You don't believe that."

"Ding ding ding," Coulson said. "And Guerra has just won the first game of *I Don't Give a Shit*. Can we go someplace where something is happening, or are we going to wander around in flower beds all night?"

There was some shuffling off in the darkness.

Guerra stopped. Held out one hand to indicate the rest of them should stop, too.

"You see a ghost?" Coulson asked, half-mockingly.

Guerra shook his head. He was hesitant to talk. Unless he was mistaken and had begun hearing phantom sounds, something was very wrong here.

"I—I heard something," Guerra said, his voice sounding somewhat hoarse in the back of his throat.

"Well, Coulson hasn't stopped talking since we got in here," Sterling replied, "so it might be that."

Coulson laughed. "Rook! Check out the biting tongue on that motherfucker."

"Both of you shut up," Guerra said.

This time when he listened, he thought he was getting some sense of where the sound had originated.

Then, something pinged off in the distance. Light reflected back at them, and this time, Guerra was confident they had all seen it.

Sahana pointed to the middle of the gardens. "I think we've found some of Dysart's handiwork."

They followed her finger and saw something in the distance.

"Are those—bodies?" Sterling asked.

The words sent chills skittering down Guerra's spine, as he felt this mission already sliding free of his control.

The mental image of himself, of someone who would rise quickly in the ranks of the UG, began to slip a little further from view, as though he had been escorted to the back row of the movie theater. Oh, he could still see the images on the screen, but they were a little more blurry, a little more unwieldy, than before.

The greasy rope keeping his guts together slipped a little, jerked taught, and he found himself reeling.

Guerra made a low sound in the back of his throat. "Fraid so," he said. "Looks to be the remains of the protest scheduled here on...Founder's Day."

"Oh, the irony," Coulson said. Then, he hawked up and spat on the ground at his feet. "Dysart better hope he's got on iron underpants, because I'm going to shove the barrel of this—"

"Stop it," Guerra said.

He took a few uneven steps forward, peering into the blackness.

"I know this is a diplomatic mission and all, but—"

"I said *stop*," Guerra said. "Stop talking."

Then, he heard something. It was faint and distant but nevertheless audible above the surrounding darkness.

Guerra made eye contact with Katarina, who nodded and crept along the garden's barrier wall. The rest of them stood at a kind of shocked attention.

Katarina snapped a familiar hand signal into the air, and each one of them turned off his or her headlamp in quick succession. The darkness, which had been ominous before, was now all-encompassing. Guerra, for one, couldn't see much of anything in front of his face, and Katarina was merely a white speck in the distance.

Eventually, even the speck disappeared.

Guerra heard small sounds, each amplified in the sensory deprivation tank that was the ARK. The low whistle of Coulson's breath in his nose—he was a famously loud-breather—and Sterling's bones shaking inside his uni.

But underneath that, he heard an even slighter sound, even more minuscule than Katarina's footsteps on the pebbles of the garden's vast walkways.

The noise, which was coming from directly in front of them, sounded eerily like...chewing.

Teeth scraping on bone. Pulling meat from sinew. Gobbling down...flesh.

His first impulse was to ask the rest of the crew if they heard it, but he thought it to be a mistake. Right now, as he stood here, that sound—that awful sound—was merely a figment of his imagination. Vocalizing it might make it real, and if it were real—he might go absolutely insane.

Then the lights came on, and all the horror in Guerra's mind suddenly became terrifyingly real.

He opened his mouth to scream—to say anything at all—and all that came out was a single, strained syllable.

"Go!"

The overhead flood lights revealed all the horror which had just moments before existed only Guerra's mind.

"Fall back! Now!"

11

Beyond the outline of Katarina's suit was a mound of flesh, not unlike the images of past wars he'd been forced to endure as a young cadet in the UG.

Bodies stacked as high as a human being were piled among the signs and guns and stage riser for the protest.

It was horrible.

Severed limbs. Decapitated heads. Eyes staring blindly, mouths agape, screaming for help that wouldn't make it in time.

It was a gruesome, hellish vision straight out of the mind of William Blake.

Or The Bible itself.

Behold, a pale horse: and his name that sat on him was Death, and Hell followed with him.

As he turned and ran, Guerra could not disentangle the images from his mind. All the blood, the death.

And the sounds: horrible, wet ripping sounds, like reams of soggy paper being torn in half, undergirded by the moans of the people—the *things*—which had caused this spilled blood.

They had turned their attention to the crew from the Arumishi as one, giant beast. A ship turning slowly in a river of blood.

But it was the *eyes* which had really bothered him.

The twinkling eyes in the darkness, *behind* the bodies. Open mouths filled with sharp teeth—covered in blood.

That was what they were running from. That was what had prompted Guerra to demand everyone abandon this massacre and return from whence they had come.

And these figures were headed right for Guerra and his crew.

Things, not people.

As the crew lumbered up the hill leading to the garden's exit—not a garden, he thought; a noxious funeral parlor—the lights above them flickered and died, leaving them in complete and utter darkness.

Not again, Guerra thought.

A myriad of sounds erupted in the wide open space, from screams to gunfire to a weird, monolithic burbling sound, a thousand open mouths creating a hungry, atonal hymn.

And then it multiplied, as though it were catching. A virus, replicating itself across the expanse of this landscape.

There was nothing Guerra or any of his cohorts could do about it —except keep running.

Katarina continued to fend off the wave of...whatever these things were, but Guerra had no illusion that it would work.

"Fall back!" he screamed, and as he turned, an explosion rocked this part of the ship. He didn't turn to see what had caused it, but in that momentary flash, he caught sight of the rest of the crew.

His crew.

But not all of them.

He saw the new kid and the cleric, but Coulson and Katarina were nowhere to be seen. Guerra fled along the far side of the street, where the glow from distant department store lights illuminated the footpath.

Make it back to the ship, he thought. Make it back to the ship, and then you can regroup, come up with a more measured plan. Running and screaming does nobody any good.

Guerra thumbed the safety off his force weapon, and once it was charged, he prepared to use it.

He knelt behind an overturned vehicle and listened for an approaching enemy. The neon glow of a mod shop gave him just enough visibility to spy one of *them* as it stepped and clicked in his direction.

There were humanoid grunts underneath the improbable consonants, but its language wasn't anything resembling human speech. Still, even though he couldn't quite figure out the origin, he refused to acknowledge the word floating in his mind's forefront.

Alien.

It's what he wanted to say. Wanted to believe. But he couldn't, because, even though they were in space, no world-shattering discoveries had been made regarding the existence of extraterrestrials.

Maybe this is it, he thought. The thing everybody's waiting for.

Until then—until he got a verification—Guerra would operate under the strict understanding that whatever they were dealing with was human.

His eyes and his gut told him otherwise, but he was a man of science—of *logic*—so he would hang onto any untested conclusions until they were verified.

Again, his mind wanted to intervene.

They were *feeding* on human *flesh*, you fucking imbecile, it said.

But he kept all that under wraps.

He returned his attention to his crew. All were accounted for, except for Coulson.

Maybe he's a goner, Guerra thought.

He peeked around the side of the overturned car and caught sight of this missions security guard.

Katarina was being hounded by a horde of—

(*the aliens*)

—these demented people, the muzzle flash of her semi-automatic weapon revealing a face etched with determination.

Every time she hit one of *them*, the figure emitted a high-pitched yowl unlike anything Guerra had ever heard.

The screaming didn't seem to bother Katarina. Then again, nothing really did. She continued firing into the crowd, doing less damage than she probably thought she should, but stopping a few here and there nonetheless.

The fact that the crowd hardly seemed fazed by it sent Guerra's stomach into pitiful convulsions.

She was firing indiscriminately into the crowd—a big no-no—and even then, it wasn't doing much of anything. She pumped round after high velocity round into their bodies, and still they kept coming.

It wasn't until she hit them in the *head* that they dropped, crumpling to the ground, and even then, they didn't stop coming. Not entirely.

His thoughts and observations were interrupted by the sight of an enemy sliding into view, moving with an inhuman fluidity he couldn't quite square with reality.

His force gun hummed in his hands. It was ready. *He* was ready. Whatever he hit with this thing, it would be turned instantly into a jellylike goo before the recipient knew what hit them.

He stood up, ready to fire—

And got knocked flat on his ass.

It took him a moment to realize he'd been sideswiped, but he didn't wait around to figure out how. He rolled to one side just in time to avoid being stomped into the concrete.

He looked up, straight into the face of one of...those things.

The tall, dark, misshapen figure tilted its head to one side and raised the foot to try again, but just then it exploded into a million bloody pieces.

When the spray of blood cleared, the two stumps that couldn't pass for legs fell over, and Coulson, gun in hand, stood in its wake.

He was smiling as though nothing had happened.

"What a fucking day to have bad reception, am I right?" he screamed.

As if in reply, Guerra's headset shrieked in his ear. Something was *definitely* wrong with it. He pulled the piece and decided to work on instinct until he reached the ship.

Just as Coulson clapped him on the back, trying to compel in forward, another one of the clicking beasts appeared behind them and grabbed Coulson by one shoulder, yanking him into the air as if he were a plushy filled with stuffing.

The darkness had lifted—lights had flickered on in and around a great many of the shops—and Guerra was treated to an up close view of their new attacker.

The good news was that it appeared on the surface to be human. The bad news? He could tell in his gut that it wasn't. This...thing, whatever it was, had been taken over by a non-human entity and was being piloted like a ship made of blood, bone, and sinew.

Guerra lowered the dose on the force gun and fired, and the thing —whatever it was—was flung backwards in an explosion of air. The blast did not rip it apart, but that benefited Coulson more than the adversary.

Guerra hurried over and helped the downed medical officer to his feet.

"Let's get out of here," Guerra said.

"No argument from me," Coulson replied, and the two fled towards the ship's exit.

He looked over his shoulder a single time, and he really wished he hadn't.

But Lot's wife looked back, and, lo, she became a pillar of salt.

The creatures had recovered from Katarina's assault—she was now running in their direction, as well—and they were advancing, moving ever closer to Guerra and the rest.

By the time Guerra reached the changing station, the others had put on their spacesuits, but he and Coulson would have no time for such luxuries. He just hoped he could hold his breath long enough to make it aboard their own ship.

Sahana opened the door, her blast gun pointed right at him, and just as she yelled, "Duck!" he did just that, and the thing right on his heels was thrown comically backward.

As he slipped into the compression chamber—everyone else was already dressed—he couldn't communicate with them but only gave them a frantic look and pointed at the ship. They appeared to be on the same page, because Sahana nodded and pressed the button that would open the door to the ship's exterior.

Open space.

Where Guerra could not breathe.

Where the temperature reached negative four hundred degrees—nearing absolute zero.

Where he would be totally unconscious within fifteen seconds, because the air would be forced from his lungs.

The creatures from the garden slammed against the door to the chamber, and even though the structure was meant to withstand destructive impacts, he didn't know how much of their attacks it would be able to endure.

He looked up just as a head-shaped dent appeared from the other side. They were going to bash their way through, even if they had to use their heads to do it.

The next moment, Katarina grabbed Guerra and told him to cling to her as she did a sort of precise run-jump toward the ship.

Things went absolutely black for some time.

∼

When he awoke again, Guerra was on the ship, and he heard a whole lot of screaming from his crew mates.

He sat up, feeling absurdly ill, and tried to get hits wits about him. The whole ship was under siege from things he was beginning to believe we're not human at all.

Meanwhile, the whole of the Arumishi was being bombarded by the fists of these inhuman entities, and Guerra felt the walls closing in on him.

All it would take was one compromised wall. One blunt-force smack to a weak seal, and they would all be dead within the minute.

He got to his feet and prepared himself for the coming onslaught. Looking out the windows and portholes in the ship, he saw that the ship was covered in the half-human creatures. They covered the ship's exterior like ants on a candy bar.

Almost immediately, he got a wry pat on the shoulder.

"You're up," Coulson said. "Good. Now, get a fucking gun and get ready. They're coming."

He did exactly that.

12

Guerra suited up and found his way to the airlock, force gun in hand.

"The fuck are you going?" Coulson asked.

"We can't wait for them to penetrate the ship for us to fight back, now can we?"

He was talking, but the words themselves felt like they were coming from somewhere far off, or like someone was using his body to say things he didn't want said.

"We have the external guns," Coulson countered. "Katarina and Sahana are on them."

"And you?" Guerra asked.

"I fucking kept you alive," Coulson said. "I was on my way to one of the exterior weapons when you woke up."

Guerra returned the shoulder pat and smiled to the best of his ability. It wasn't great, but it would do in a pinch.

"Thanks," he said. "Now, I'm going outside the craft to see what I can do. You want to go, just follow me. But don't try to stop me, or else."

Coulson seemed on the verge of saying something, but in the end he just nodded. "Let's go," he said, and they did just that.

They hurried to the rear of the ship and began the process of getting ready to leave the Arumishi.

He would normally have to be in airlock for several minutes in a pressurized suit, breathing pure oxygen and eliminating the nitrogen from his body.

But he didn't have time for that.

They needed to be outside, knocking these slobbering monsters off the side of their ship.

And so he'd have to risk his health. It was the least he could do to get them out of here.

His elbows and knees already felt like shit, so this would only make things worse, but if they didn't fend off this monstrous attack, all the oxygen in the world wouldn't make him feel better in the long run.

"This is fucking pointless," Coulson said. "If we go out there, we're fucking dead men."

"And if we don't?" Guerra asked.

For the first time in their brief acquaintance, Guerra saw genuine emotion in Coulson's eyes.

"We're probably fucking dead men," he said.

And he meant it, too. Guerra knew that.

He realized, then, they were going to flood the ship. They didn't have a snowball's chance in hell of turning them back.

At this point, they were only delaying the inevitable.

When they reached the airlock, they found The Cap working on it, him leaning over some machine or another, his whole body covered in sweat.

"Get to the deck," he said. "We need to get the hell out of here."

"Copy that," Cap replied, "but I've already initiated the warm-up sequence. I hate to tell you, but it's going to take time. This baby's older than most of you, and she takes a minute to reach her peak."

"Get that goddamned bay door shut, at the very least, then."

Cap turned and looked at Guerra. "We're missing one, bossman."

"Who?"

Guerra did a quick mental attendance check on the crew, and his heart sank.

Sterling, the new guy, was nowhere to be seen.

Oh, no, Guerra thought.

It was then he saw a figure bursting through a line of the yellow-eyed figures down by the landing pad, and the figure was wearing one of the standard UG suits.

"Sterling," he screamed into the mic, but he knew it wasn't getting through. He just hoped the kid knew he needed to hurry up.

Sterling got tangled in a group of shambling figures, and he clumsily turned and fired the force gun into a crowd of them. One bleeding, red-skinned attacker exploded into pieces, but the rest remained mostly intact.

Except, that wasn't the end of it.

The dismembered figure continued to struggle even after it was on the ground, and Sterling had to high-step over the thing to get to the ship. His eyes full of panic, he dropped his weapon and leaped without looking.

"Cap!" he screamed, "get on the deck and get us the hell out of here."

"But the--"

"I said *go*," Guerra replied, and the Captain receded into the depths of the ship. Moments later, a low, rattling hum fired up beneath them. The ship then rose slowly from the edge of the ARK platform, and for a moment there, it looked like they would get away.

Sterling clung to one of the ship's landing skids, which he wouldn't be able to hang onto for very long.

But if they could just get out of the attackers' jumping range, then they could open the bay door and pull the kid in.

Just then, a *giant* figure leaped onto the edge of the landing platform and clamped one meaty hand around Sterling's ankle.

Under the weight of the hulking attacker, the ship tilted sideways, and Coulson and Guerra began to slide out.

Guerra pressed one foot against the wall and reached forward, grabbing Sterling by the wrist.

Coulson wasn't as lucky. He want sliding forward, hands-first, right out the bay door.

Guerra, who was holding Sterling's wrist, used his other hand to clamp down on Coulson's boot.

He felt the immediate pull on both shoulders, and they would be yanked from the sockets any second now.

Goddamned gravity, he thought. Inside the landing bay, there was a modicum of gravity, even if the atmosphere was all space. The physics didn't make sense to Guerra, but science wasn't his expertise.

The ship had titled to a sixty degree angle, which threatened to upend the whole gang and send them plummeting back down to the ship's outer lip.

Guerra craned his neck to see Katarina aiming her force gun just above his head, and he panicked. It wasn't a precision weapon. It normally behaved more like a shotgun than a sniper rifle—unless you changed the settings—and anything in the immediate vicinity would be torn to pieces.

He sincerely hoped she wasn't willing to sacrifice them all for the sake of survival, but if it had to be, it had to be.

Guerra tried to leverage himself so he could pull up, but the ship was too busy getting weighed down and pulled to the wrong side.

It as then he got a good look at one of these—things.

The big guy, the giant, was a mass of sinewy muscle and a kind of gelatinous outer coating, like someone soaked in a thick, reused motor oil. He wasn't *undead*, like a zombie, so much as he had *transformed* into a different being entirely.

The ship labored under the weight of the giant, and other like figures followed suit, latching onto the ship and trying to hold it in place. The thrusters weren't strong enough to counter this offensive. It was but a seeker vessel intended for small-range missions.

Low conflict.

Not this.

"Katarina," Guerra screamed, hoping the assassin was close enough to hear, "forget the kills. Help. Us."

Her gun, poised for a kill shot, faltered, and she glanced down at

Guerra, who was thankful to see she had adopted a sane expression. She'd been cursed with a volatile temper, but instead of sacrificing them for her bloodlust, she sheathed the blast gun and squatted down to help out.

She pulled forcefully on Guerra's ankle and helped him back into the ship, which, in turn, pulled the rest of the crew back up. Even Sterling, who appeared like he might become the first casualty in the crew, managed to find safety.

Then, just as they seemed to get their bearings, the giant pulled himself up onto the side and into the ship—and others followed.

They had made it aboard. If enough of them flung themselves at the ship—

"Put the ship down," Guerra yelled into his helmet mic.

All he got from the other end was static, and though he repeated his command—even louder this time—he didn't get a response from Cap.

The next thing he knew, he was being slammed against the wall. His whole body shook with the force of the giant's hand pressing against him, and he hung onto consciousness by the thinnest of membranes.

"Just shoot," he said, wheezing into the mic. He couldn't see Katarina or Coulson or even the kid, but he hoped to God one of them would take out the beast before it destroyed the whole ship.

The beast punched him, trying to get through the glass and the film of his helmet to the meat beneath.

He was slammed one more time against the wall, but something about this felt different. Guerra didn't have much left of whatever was keeping him alive, but he was determined not to let go just yet.

There was a moment of confusion—a loud, chaotic moment in which he anticipated approaching death—but then, when he looked up, he realized he was on the ground, and the giant was on top of him, the whole of its weight bearing down on him, threatening to crush him.

He glanced up into its face and saw that the beast's dim-eyed expression and realized it was dead.

As he brought himself back from the brink, Coulson pulled him out from underneath the smelly, goo-covered corpse. Coulson was wide-eyed and panting but otherwise fine.

Katarina, meanwhile, was blasting away on the ship's few remaining creatures. The kid—Sterling—was cowering in the corner, holding his hands over his head.

Oh, well, Guerra thought. I'm going to ignore that, for now.

Guerra hurt all over, but he was still alive, so he wouldn't complain.

Katarina finished off the last of the invading creatures—Guerra couldn't stand to think of them as *people*—and then they all watched in horror as a bisected form crawled toward her.

Her foot came down—and came down again—until the thing stopped moving. It gave a high-pitched sigh and then settled down to die.

When all was still—inside, at least—Katarina looked at Guerra and Coulson and said, simply, "Fu-uck."

13

They found the Captain and his second-in-command on the flight deck, desperately working on some mechanical thing or another to keep the ship airborne.

"It's like flies on shit out there," the Captain said. "We're completely covered in those fucking things. We couldn't take off if I had a rocket jammed up my ass."

"And getting worse by the moment, by the look of it," Coulson said, peering out the main window.

The rest of them were standing next to the Captain. Hands on hips, contemplating what to do next.

Sterling, meanwhile, was again sitting in the corner. Knees to chest, head in his arms. Guerra thought but could not be certain he was not whimpering like a small dog.

"What are those things, rich boy?" Coulson said. "Is this some kind of ARK army? Their Imperial Guard or something? What the fuck *are* they?"

When the kid didn't answer, Coulson kicked him. Nothing hard; just a swift swipe to the leg.

"Leave him alone," Sahana said. "He's freaking out."

"*He's* freaking out?" Coulson replied. "*I'm* freaking out. We should *all* be freaking out, if we know what's good for us. These things are going to crack open the ship like a candy bar, and we're the gooey caramel right dead center of it."

"Kicking him isn't going to do any good," Sahana replied, and Coulson raised a hand, pointing at her, intending on replying, when Sterling finally spoke.

"It's the mods," he said. "They've all been driven crazy by the stuff in all those shops."

"That's not crazy," Coulson replied. "*I'm* crazy. That out there—that's something way fucking *beyond* crazy. They look like slicked-up, roided out freaks. Whatever they are, it's not human, and it sure as hell ain't just a little mental illness."

Sterling got up. "They're human," he said. "It's the dosing. Their biological make-ups have been changed by whatever they were taking. That imbalance is what has driven them to this point. That scene back at the garden, that is what I suspect we'd see all throughout the ship."

"And how, exactly, do you know this?"

The kid looked sullen. "Just trust me, all right. I know what I'm talking about."

"He's studied Xenograd."

"Yeah, plus I have eyes," Sterling responded.

Speaking of eyes, Guerra thought, there was nothing but fear in the kid's face. He wasn't ready for this kind of mission, and as soon as they got back to the UG's main ship, he was going to tell anyone and everyone who would listen. He didn't *care* who the kid's parents were.

But first, they had to survive this debacle.

The thud of feet on the ship's outer hull sounded like bowling ball-sized hail. Their attackers—

(*aliens*)

(*zombies*)

(*monsters*)

—were swarming like ants, and there was nothing they could do but sit and wait, hoping to whatever God was out there that they might make it off the ARK and back into the distant realm of space.

One step ahead of Guerra, the Captain turned and said, "We can't take off like this. There's just too many of these goddamned things on us. It'll just short-circuit the engine and the thrusters. We don't have enough juice to push off."

"Call the base," Guerra replied. "Let's get reinforcements. Then we can regroup while the UG comes up with a plan."

"No can do," the Captain replied. "Those things out there—in their infinite wisdom—have chewed up the comms device. Although, to be honest, I don't remember it working terribly well beforehand."

They listened in silent, horrified awe at the sound of the beings on the ship's outer hull.

Thudda-thudda-thump.

It was like a slow-motion riot. Guerra peered through the nearest port hole, which was teeming with body parts, all wriggling and writhing in an attempt to get at the ship's gooey center—just like Coulson had said.

"I wish we had a fucking cattle prod," Coulson said. "Then we could herd the bastards back into their own goddamned ship."

Then, the Captain's eyes lit up.

"Wait a second," he said. "I have an idea. It's not a prod, *per se*, but it'll do the trick. Come with me. I'll need some help."

Guerra followed the Captain through the ship, where the rest of the crew was huddled, each coping with this human asteroid shower in his or her own way.

Sahana sat cross-legged in her chair, eyes closed and breath passing slowly in and out of her lungs. Katarina, naturally, sat emotionless along the sideboard, her hand holding a pistol like a comfort blanket.

Sterling, of course, peered nervously after them but did not follow. He seemed, well, not content, exactly, in the ship's inner sanctum, but safe at the very least.

The Cap's second-in-command, Aiden, tugged at the neck of his red vest and said, "I hope you're not planning on—"

"I am," the Captain said, turning once to leer at the younger version of himself following on his heels.

"What's going on?" Guerra asked, as they traveled deeper into the ship's belly.

Aiden answered. "He's going to short out a specific part of the main electrical system, which will send a hard jolt to the ship's outer frame."

"Sounds dangerous," Guerra replied.

"It is," the Captain said. "But it will most likely get these sons-of-bitches off of us, and then we can take off."

"*If* we can take off," said the second-in-command.

"We can take off, goddamnit," Cap replied. "You just get your ass back to the bridge and prepare to shove off, you hear me?"

Aiden looked like he wanted to say something, but instead, he turned and headed back toward the front of the ship.

Above them, the hungry thumping continued. Guerra's pulse quickened by a handful of beats, but he kept his focus on the Captain, tried to remain calm under the idea that the old man knew what he was doing.

But he had his questions.

The Captain kicked a panel off the wall and pulled out a set of wire cutters. He then yanked a set of yellow cables out of the wall and held the blades to them.

"Brace yourself," he told Guerra, and then, into his mic, he said, "Let me know when you're ready."

There was a hearty sigh on the other end, but then the second-in-command said, "If you're going to do this, do it now."

And he did.

The Captain clipped the wires.

14

The resulting electrical shock slammed Guerra against the nearest wall with bone-cracking force, his body feeling like it had been tempered in lightning. His head smacked something hard and metal, and consciousness eluded him for several moments.

When he reopened his eyes, a high-pitched hum had settled in his ears. He pushed himself groggily to his feet and helped the Captain to his.

They stood in silent wonder for a few moments, each of them listening. Instead of the clatter of hundreds of feet stomping on the outside of the ship, Guerra heard...nothing.

Silence.

Nada.

"*Mierda*," he said. "I can't believe it."

"It worked," the Captain said, his shocked face sliding into a broad smile, and then he screamed, "It fucking worked! I didn't think it would, but it fucking worked!"

He danced a little jig to the nearest porthole and peered out.

Guerra joined him and witnessed a scene that gave him hope.

Outside, amidst the darkness, hundreds and hundreds of bodies floated off into space, toward some unknown destination. Some of them seemed pretty damned unhappy about it—they flailed their arms and screamed into the void—but it looked like none of them remained on the ship.

"That looks to be all of them," Guerra said, astounded. "Obviously, we'll have to take stock of the ship and finish off any remaining...things, but for the most part—"

"You leave that up to me and my minion!" the Captain said. He was absolutely ecstatic, and Guerra had to give it to him: he absolutely had the right to be.

Guerra followed him back to the flight deck, where the rest of the crew was recuperating. Katarina was leaning against the controls, and Sahana remained fixed in her pose of silent contemplation. Coulson was holding his head and cursing, but he was no more injured than before.

Sterling, on the other hand, was curled up in a ball on the floor. He had the look of someone who had *seen some shit*. The only problem was, so had they. He should be in no worse shape than the rest of them.

"What now?" Guerra asked the Captain.

The Captain said, "All I have to do is go outside and reconfigure a little wiring, and then *bam!*—we're back on the road."

Guerra surveyed the scene. "Not a moment too soon."

Sterling sat up and said, his voice quavering, "Don't go out there. It's not—it's not safe."

The Captain pointed to the mostly dead figures floating across the wide expanse of space. "They're not getting back to us unless they can shit fire," he said.

"Could the ship take off without you going outside?" Guerra asked. "I mean, is it possible?"

The second-in-command rolled his eyes and said, "No. We're going to have to go out on the top of this beast and reconfigure some things to be able to blast off. Until then, you will all have to wait and be patient. This will take a while."

"It was worth it. Otherwise, we'd be still scratching our heads, looking for a way out of this fucking pickle."

"He's not wrong," Coulson said, rubbing his temples. "I thought we were going to be those things' fucking *lunch*."

Sahana, opening her eyes, said, "I don't advise it."

The Captain *almost* looked perturbed. "And why the fuck not?"

"There is nothing good outside the walls of this ship," Sahana replied. "You go outside, and you put us *all* at risk."

The Captain smiled. "Thank you for your vote of confidence, mystic, but I have a duty to obey more than my own moral and philosophical intuition. I've got an actual boss to answer to. And besides, if I don't go out there and jury-rig the electronics, we're not going *anywhere*."

The cleric's countenance never changed. "It is possible for us to be found without risking our lives. We survived once. If we open the door again, it will not be a destitute country we invite in, but Hell itself."

The Captain waved her off and disappeared down a nearby corridor.

Coulson took up his skepticism, without missing a beat. "So, what do you expect us to do, wait here for rescue?"

"The UG knows we're here," Sahana said. "Even without our comms systems, they have no choice but to come look for us. We have provisions enough to last us for a few days."

Coulson leered at her. "Meanwhile, we sit out here like fucking sardines waiting to be plucked out and devoured? No, thank you. Plus, the ship is *toast*. Who knows what will happen if we just sit here and twiddle our thumbs?"

Katarina cleared her throat and said, "Going inside is the only way out."

Coulson's whole face turned red. "Back in there with the fucking lunatic cannibals? Have you lost your goddamned *mind*? Have you been huffing the force gun fumes?"

Cap reappeared briefly. "Don't get your boxers in a bunch. We won't need to go inside that hellhole again. Just—I'm telling you, just give me a flipping minute, and we'll have the ship as good as new."

Aiden said, "Or something to that degree."

The Captain smiled. "Wish me luck," he said.

Aiden, ever the loyal servant, pushed the button to open the bay door. The arm sparked to life and pulled the door up.

At first, Guerra couldn't see the thing that crawled under the opening, but by the time he did, it was too late to do anything about it.

Whatever it was only vaguely resembled a human being, and when it reared up on its hind quarters, it resembled a scorpion or some kind of arthropodal creature. It still had the features of a human being—a face and torso and ostensible arms—but it was as though some mad scientist had taken a person apart and reassembled him as a monster.

At full height, it was a head taller than any person in the crew, including Katarina, who was already a head taller than anyone else.

Guerra, lunging forward, kicked at it, but the thing was too quick. It slithered sideways and reared up again and unfurled one of its claw-like arms. Just as the thing swung at Aiden, the victim attempted to step out of the way.

He was a moment too late.

The sharp end point of the arm pierced the second-in-command right above the breast bone, sliding through him like hot metal through butter. The action was punctuated by a bright green spray and a scream that would haunt even the most battle-hardened soldier.

Aiden's eyes popped open and his mouth wrenched into a silent scream. His hands gripped frantically at the claw in his chest but managed to do no good in displacing it.

Fortunately, Katarina had seen it all. She had snatched up a two-shot weapon—sometimes called a *boom shot*—and unloaded both barrels into the scorpion figure's chest.

Blood and gore of an unknown variety splattered inside the rear deck, the smell like smoke mixed with a vinegar rising from the floor where the bodies lay.

But Katarina wasn't done. She slid a dagger free of her belt and swiped upward, slicing the claw arm in two. The thing emitted a high-pitched, animalistic squeal and backed away.

Meanwhile, the Captain had stepped beyond the ship's threshold, out into space, the clang of his boots on the rungs of the outer ladder audible well inside the ship.

"Jesus Christ," the Captain said into his headset. "Kill that fucking thing while I get us up and running."

The door began to close.

"Come back here," Guerra yelled into his mic, but it did no good. The Captain was already halfway up the ladder.

Coulson, who stood in a kind of shocked silence, stepped forward as if to hurdle past the thing and join the Captain outside.

But the scorpion beast kept coming.

The thing let out a lower growl and skittered to one side of the ship. It wasn't just a blind automaton, working by instinct. There appeared to be some strategy to its vicious attack, which terrified Guerra to no end.

As all this was happening, Aiden lay slumped against the far wall, burbling like an aging coffee maker. Blood seeped from his mouth, and the gaping, checkmark-shaped wound in his chest spouted blood like a spigot had come loose.

No one in this crew was expendable. One of the reasons they brought this small a force was that each person had a function, and Aiden's was clear: he had to keep the trains running on time, so to speak. The Captain was the captain, of course, but Aiden knew really what was going down.

Guerra made a move toward the downed second-in-command, perhaps in an effort to stanch the bleeding, but Katarina, placing her dagger directly in front of him, stopped him dead in his tracks.

She shook her head. "He's a goner," Katarina said. "Leave him be."

The next moment, she was a blur, blitzing toward the monster in their midst.

She disassembled the scorpion beast in a matter of moments. A *sous chef* couldn't have made quicker work of the thing's limbs. That neon green fluid sprayed the walls, and Guerra and the rest ducked as Katarina finished it off.

When at last she lowered her blade, she was covered in the sticky, foul-smelling material.

But she didn't waste any time. She knelt down and placed herself in the beast's eye-line. With just a head remaining, the thing *almost* looked human.

"Can you understand me?" she said. "You move like an animal, but you think like a person. Can you hear me?"

The thing smiled vaguely but did not answer.

Sahana stepped in and knelt next to it. When she placed one purple hand on the figure's brow, it flinched, and then something like humanity passed over its face.

"I can hear you," the mystic said, interpreting the thing's thoughts, "and soon, you will hear us. All of us. And what we have to say is—death is preferable to the alternative."

15

Sahana looked up to see the rest of the crew gaping at her. Guerra didn't quite know how to react, but he knew he was about at his limit.

"She cannot help what she is doing," the mystic said.

The thing at their feet said something else, and Sahana nodded. She said, "And she is in great pain."

"No shit, lady," Coulson said. "Our female assassin just took off all her arms and legs. She *should* be in pain."

Guerra stepped forward. "Coulson—"

"No," Coulson replied. "Ask her how she feels about putting a fucking *tentacle* through one of our crew mates. Huh? Do you want to ask her that?"

Sahana was on her feet before Coulson could react. "You may not respect the lives of all living things," she said, "but I *do*. So, if you are going to disrespect this creature, you will not do so in my presence."

"Katarina," Coulson said, speaking over Sahana's shoulder, "put this thing out of our misery, will you?"

But Katarina didn't move, and neither did Sahana. Guerra watched the tense exchange with interest but did not interfere.

"I understand your frustration," Sahana said, "but if you are this aggressive in her presence, she will tell us nothing."

"So far as I know, she's still told us nothing."

"She said she's no monster. She said *they* turned her into this."

"Oh yeah?"

"There is the potential for her to give us valuable information about what went on inside that ship," Sahana replied.

"And she communicated all of this to you with her fucking *mind*?" Coulson asked. "Are you fucking crazy?"

Sahana smirked. "Maybe a little," she replied.

Coulson seemed to bite his lip. He glanced from the group to the dead figure on the ground at the monster's feet.

"Fuck this," Coulson said. "I'm going to help the Captain. I can't let what happened to Aiden happen to him. We'll *never* get off this floating death trap, otherwise."

And then he was off, dragging a human-sized rifle with him.

At least they would get out of here, he thought. At least they would be able to take what they had seen back with them and report that the leader of the ARK had finally, truly lost his goddamned mind.

Guerra sat on the nearest bench.

He was tired. Didn't know what to do. They couldn't contact the main ship at the UG. This was a clusterfuck. They'd have him riding a desk in the deepest, darkest corner of the worst office, whichever that one was.

In the meantime, he watched Sahana commune with the half-human figure at their feet. Aiden's body still seemed to be leaking blood, but he showed zero signs of life.

He was gone as soon as he hit the ground.

Such a waste. Aiden was a promising addition to the United Galaxy. Once he got out from underneath the Captain, he would have *gone* places. Might have become one of the youngest people the pilot a ship in the UG's fleet.

The look on the kid's face turned his stomach. His face stared blankly, questioningly into the distance. As if he were unsure of the truth of what had occurred.

How could this happen to me, the face seemed to say.

I can't take this, Guerra thought.

He got up and found a nearby sheet to cover the kid with. Once they were on the ride back home, he'd transport the body to the medical bay and stay with Aiden until they reached their home ship. It was the least he could do. It was his *duty* to do so.

And then, the wry, villainous voice at the back of his mind began to pick at him, to scrape at the scab of his insecurities, hoping he'd bleed all over himself in front of the crew.

You're not *going* back, the voice said. Look out that window. That will be you. You and the rest of your...crew.

Shut up, Guerra thought, but the thought held no weight.

Guerra, being raised in a household that respected the old laws, the ways which had given people hope in the days when they lived on Earth, he was prone to an outmoded version of American Exceptionalism.

His parents prayed on Sundays and did no work. Even on a ship far from their original home, they felt close to the Higher Power they felt watched over them.

As a matter of faith, Guerra followed similar beliefs. He was sure there was *something* out there protecting them.

He just didn't know if he felt it *himself*.

Growing up, his parents being so thoroughly enveloped in The Spirit, he was able to coast on their utter devotion.

Now that he was an adult—now that he was facing his own crisis of faith—he could not cling to what his parents believed. He had to stand on his own two feet and assert the knowledge that he felt protected by something greater than himself.

But he didn't.

That was the problem.

He felt an absence, really, for the first time in his life. There was just a hollow spot where the faith of his childhood had been, and he didn't know how to fill it.

And if he couldn't fill it, he couldn't lead. He couldn't inspire others, and he certainly push them through...well, whatever this was.

A creeping sense of doom overwhelmed him, and he thought increasingly about giving up, about letting someone else—maybe not Coulson—take over and guide them through this.

He looked up and saw the others looking at him.

He breathed, and he breathed again.

Somehow, he felt better.

Once the Captain gets back, he thought, placating the furious anger of the thing inside of him, we'll go on our merry way, and this will soon be nothing more than a terrible nightmare.

Oh, it'll be a terrible nightmare all right, the voice said, but you won't be getting on your way anytime soon. Just listen out. See what happens to the Captain.

His self-directed anger subsided when he heard the sound of the Captain's feet on the rungs outside the ship.

Maybe it's going to be all right, after all.

See there, you son-of-a-bitch, he told the voice.

The voice—which was basically himself.

But time passed, and no one banged on the door outside, so Guerra hurried over to open the bay, his heart beating an uneven jazz rhythm in his chest.

Where is the Captain? he wondered, hoping the question would be answered *for* him.

But the low feeling in his stomach made him wonder if he *wanted* to know the answer.

When the button was pressed and the bay door ratcheted up, Guerra could not quite believe his eyes.

16

Guerra opened his mouth to scream, but no sound came out. The sight had stolen his breath from him, and so he could only choke on the air that would not come.

The Captain was dead.

Worse than dead.

He was in two pieces, bisected across the midsection where his backbone met his hips.

It was a clean, nearly bloodless cut, but it did the trick. Cap had managed to stay secured to the side of the ship, but he was as dead as his second-in-command.

Where's your fucking faith *now*, boy?

The voice again. Taunting him. Trying to drive him to make a mistake. To let them in.

He could almost hear this voice aside and apart from himself, but he didn't worry about that.

Not yet—not now.

Before something else could get in there with him, he closed the bay door, lost his balance, and slid to the ground.

Coulson was the first to ask the question.

"Where the fuck is the Captain?"

Guerra didn't have the heart to tell him. His mouth opened to form the words, but the words—like everything else today—failed him.

Still, it only took a moment for him—for all of them—to come to a significantly precise conclusion.

Then Katarina put his feelings—and their collective despair—into words.

"Fuck *no*. Fuck fuck fuck *no*."

Meanwhile, Coulson was off on the other side of the ship, absolutely losing his mind. He paced the landing bay, his suit covered in blood.

"Any idea of how we fix the fucking ship?" he asked, his voice a half-octave higher than normal.

No one answered. No one even bothered to look up. Because no one did. The two people on this mission who actually had any mechanical expertise were dead.

That didn't stop the questions. Coulson continued his assault on their sense of hopelessness.

"Anyone at least know how to *fly* the goddamned thing?"

Again, there was no answer.

"And our main radio is completely fucked, right?" Coulson was practically hemorrhaging rage, at this point. "That was what the old fart used to fry the fuckers, wasn't it?"

Guerra made eye contact with Coulson, but he couldn't confirm it with words. The best he could manage was a solemn nod of the head.

In retrospect, it all seemed so silly, so stupid. *Why*, in God's name, would they do such a thing? In what universe was it an acceptable reason to destroy their comms device?

"So," Coulson said, summarizing, "we are stuck in a craft no one can fly—one that we are not even sure *can* fly—with no way to contact our main vessel. All the while, we are stationed outside a ship filled with drug-addled monsters who want to—what?— feed on us? On our *brains*?"

The hum of the undisturbed electronics was all that could be heard in the silence left by Coulson's observation.

"That's—that's about right," Guerra managed. "More or less."

Coulson smirked sardonically. "More or less? That's fucking—that's fucking *perfect*. Goddamn."

Coulson spat between his feet. Sahana knelt next to the armless scorpion creature, trying to communicate with it. Katarina dropped her head, looking between her knees, and Sterling sobbed deep in his throat.

Guerra wasn't a gambling man, but if he had to pick which one of them would probably go next, it would have to be the new guy.

And he suddenly hoped Sahana could not read *his* mind, because he was ashamed of the thoughts that lingered there.

"At least we know the truth, now, right?" Guerra said. "It can't get any worse for us, so long as we know we have one hell of an uphill battle ahead of us."

Now that it was all out in the open, maybe they could move on. Figure out some other plan, some alternative tactic for finding their way back to the UG ship.

That was, until Coulson did what he did next, because that seemed to be a clear demarcation line between hope and despair.

Coulson, brimming with rage, walked over to where the body of the intruder lay—the one which had killed Aiden—and he stomped on it.

When that didn't satisfy him, he did it again.

And again.

He stomped until he was done with the thing, until the crazed smile on his face disappeared beneath a thick sheen of green, discolored blood.

No one did anything to stop him. They just watched, because it would be folly to step in when someone was that far gone.

Sahana glared holes into Coulson but said nothing.

At first.

The medic, covered in the thing's vibrant blood, turned toward them, smiled once, almost in apology, and then ventured back into the heart of the ship.

"Well," Guerra said.

"Well, *now* we are fucked," Sahana replied, losing her mystical tone for a moment, taking on the persona of the man who had just stomped their one link to the ship's inner sanctum into a fine, bloody paste.

As if to underline this feat, she repeated herself. "We are so fucked," she said.

Coulson, perhaps hearing just how unimpressed Sahana was with his display, returned to where they were huddled.

"We're fucked *now*?" Coulson asked. "*Now*, we're fucked? How about two minutes ago? How about the moment we stepped foot on that goddamned ship?"

"I told you not to," Sahana said, calm as she'd ever been.

"But killing this fucking monster is what doomed us?" Coulson answered.

"Yes," Sahana said. "We have violated something fundamental in the role we play in the balance of things."

Coulson rolled his eyes. "Oh yeah?"

"It has tipped over and spilled something awful in our direction. It is going to pour, hot and scalding, all over us."

"The fuck outta here," Coulson responded, but Sahana wasn't done.

"We will beg for the torment to stop," she continued, "but it won't. We will be reduced to ash and bone before we are tossed aside. This —this is just the beginning."

Coulson seemed rattled, fundamentally rattled in a way he hadn't been before. Guerra watched the way his eyes changed. It was like he was a little boy again.

Like the first time a child sees a bee and realizes it could sting him. Like something had gotten through his armor.

"How do you know that?"

"The same way I knew we shouldn't have gone in the ARK and disturbed the people of Xenograd. I just know."

"Fucking great. Just fucking great."

Guerra finally spoke up.

"I told all of you it was a bad idea to go unbidden into the ARK," he said. "It broke protocol, and now we are incapable of getting out of here."

"It was just a roundabout way of doing our jobs," Coulson said. "You know. Saving people. Promoting democracy. That kind of shit."

"It was not doing your *job* at all," Guerra replied. "It was a cavalier move, and we are lucky we didn't lose *more* members of the crew in that onslaught."

Coulson smirked bitterly. "Well, if it makes you feel any better, the two most important people to this mission got killed in the onslaught."

Guerra gave him a death stare.

Coulson said, "So, at least there's that."

17

Guerra sat, head in hands, until the rest of the crew exited the bay, and then he sat there some more, as he contemplated their next path forward.

He couldn't think of anything.

And it was then he became awash in a severe bout of melancholy. It was as though everything he'd thought he would accomplish today had come crashing down in a single, deadly event.

He sighed and looked up.

From his current vantage point, he could see the ARK through a porthole.

It was a massive structure. Thousands upon thousands of rooms, housing even more people.

The sight of it suddenly made him sick to his stomach.

So much potential for violence.

And if the recent onslaught were any indication, Dysart and his government were capable of plenty.

It was possible—but not probable—that this was some kind of horrible accident.

A disease running wild through the population. A pandemic,

maybe. Something like the one disease that nearly took out humanity toward the end.

He almost smiled.

Whatever that was—whatever had infected those people—it was not the traditional sickness that took down swaths of people in disaffected countries.

It was governmental malfeasance of the highest order. That, or some major institutional neglect.

And then the glass was shattered for him.

He wondered just how many ships were operating under a similar kind of darkness. How many ignored pandemic outbreaks, or systematically undermined its citizenry?

How many *enslaved* its inhabitants?

If the UG was actually so feckless that it couldn't prevent *this* kind of genocide, then what good was it?

Moreover, what good was *he*?

Once the despair had subsided and he was more or less okay, he did the work of standing up.

That was the hard part—standing up.

If he could get to his feet, he could move forward. That was always the struggle, wasn't it? Getting up when you had been knocked down?

When he finally convinced his legs to hold him, he traced one finger on the wall as he made his way to the flight deck.

∼

HE EXPECTED the crew to be overwhelmed by grief, to be completely despondent, but they weren't.

They were *preparing*.

They were talking. Arguing over alternative plans. Judging which ones passed muster and which ones didn't.

In short, they were leading *themselves*.

They were not completely and utterly beaten down, and Guerra had to respect that.

It was like they didn't even need him.

He didn't have much time to ponder the idea, because Coulson, still hyped on his own adrenaline, was pacing the flight deck.

He said, "The mind-reader here just dropped an *epic* revelation on us."

"What's that?"

Coulson looked from Guerra to Sahana. His face was still covered in the blood which had been spilled in the act of stomping someone —or something—to death.

"There's something I neglected to share before," Sahana said. "It has to do with—with the intruder lying back in the exit bay."

"O—kay," Guerra responded.

He didn't quite know how to proceed. The rest of the crew was staring at him expectantly, like children waiting for the oldest sibling to take the blame for something he clearly did not do.

"She—*It*," Sahana continued, "did not speak the same dialect of Xenish the common people on the ARK tend to speak."

His heartbeat accelerated.

"Which means?"

He knew the answer, but he wasn't ready to hear it, so he stalled by having someone else explain it for him while he caught his breath.

This was big.

Sterling cleared his throat. "Which means Xenograd is likely transporting in people for various forms of exploitation."

Guerra looked from the kid to Sahana, who nodded. It was a slight gesture, but it was all he needed from the mystic, who was trustworthy in all aspects of diplomacy.

She wouldn't say anything she didn't believe to be the truth, and so if she thought Xenograd was hiding immigrants—or using them for some arcane, unsavory purpose—he believed her.

Guerra felt a red hot anger rise up the center of his chest and settle in his throat, right behind his voice box.

"How does that make you feel?" he asked Coulson.

"I don't feel anything at all."

"Nothing."

"Nothing," Coulson confirmed. "I did the best I could with what I knew at the time."

"God."

"Listen," Coulson said, "those things we just blasted off the ship—they're not human."

Guerra rolled his eyes. "Coulson, they—"

"They're *not*, Guerra," he said, this time more forcefully. "They were human at some point, but the thing that killed the Captain—it's something else entirely."

Guerra directed his next question to the whole crew. "And what do you think about this?"

No one could meet his gaze—except for Katarina.

"What do you think, Kat?" Guerra asked. "I know it isn't your thing to engage in strategic planning—or whatever—but what's your take?"

Katarina's gaze was steely and intrepid.

"I've killed far more vulnerable people for far less cause," she said. "I've killed for money, and I've killed for country. Now I kill for the safety of the galaxy, and if that means breaking a few eggs to ensure the safety of a whole ship, I am honored to swing the executioner's blade."

Guerra thought about it.

"So let's say we go back in there and get attacked," he said, "we'll basically be mowing down powerless victims of this regime? Is that what we're saying?"

"That's pretty—what do you call it—reductionist," Coulson replied. "Tell him, Sterling."

Sterling looked like he'd swallowed a melon. "I—I don't have anything to add to this part of the conversation."

"We're out of our depth here," Guerra said. "We don't have the clearance to—"

"*Fuck* clearance," Coulson replied. "We have righteous fucking anger, and if we can get the UG down here to take a gander at this assault on humanity, then we'd be doing net good, right?"

Guerra understood where Coulson was coming from—and the

core of him agreed—but what Coulson was ignoring was just how powerful intergalactic red tape could be. If they stepped just beyond the scope of this mission, then Xenograd would have just cause to challenge any sanctions the UG would lay on them. Which would mean a slap on the wrist, and so the ship's injustices would continue.

That wasn't all.

The other troubling part of this whole situation was that Dysart—if he were like any other tyrant Guerra knew—would begin to work tirelessly to cover his tracks the *moment* he thought his bad deeds had been discovered.

Nothing would be off the table. Document tampering. Bulk jailings. Mass genocide. By the time peace could be secured on-board, who knew how many dead or dying would be unaccounted for.

But it was now clear they could *not* do nothing. The wave had already begun to crest, and it would soon be crashing on the shore of this whole situation.

Still, he needed to be sure.

His gaze turned toward whom he believed to be his most trusted advisor on this mission. "Sahana?"

She shook her head. "I still see a mass of clouds and thunderstorms on the horizon, if we go inside that place."

"Can you be any more clear than that?"

"If we go in there," Sahana said, "we won't all walk out of there."

Guerra sighed.

"And we aren't going to try to repair the comms device?"

Coulson smirked. "Do you think *any* of us have the mechanical know-how to pull that off? I certainly don't. Do *you*, Katarina?"

She shook her head.

"Sahana?"

She seemed dubious, but she had no choice but to shake her head. "We're stuck in here."

Guerra considered it.

"But you think we'd be safest here?"

Coulson didn't give Sahana a chance to answer.

"They'll come back," he said, "and rip open this ship like an MRE.

We'd be just a fucking—a fucking *snack* to them. Yeah, yeah. And if we manage to call the UG here, they'll be the main course."

"So it's this ship or that one?"

There was an old story Guerra had read called *The Lady or the Tiger*. Behind one door, a beautiful lady. Behind the other, a vicious tiger.

This was similar, only it was more like *The Tiger or The Tiger*.

Which tiger would he choose?

Sahana's head dropped the moment before he answered.

It was like she knew.

"We're going back in," Guerra said.

And that was that.

18

This time, when they entered the ARK, they were greeted by a multitude of lights. As though the red carpet had been rolled out for them.

Up close, Xenograd looked a hell of a lot different than it had in the briefing docs. (Certainly better than it did in the dark.)

Guerra was no student of architecture, but he knew the ARK was done in a style common to the twentieth century. It was all façades and marble plaques and reinforced concrete, which—to him, at least—implied tedium, but Xenograd was awash in color. Where there was fabric, floral patterns and splashes of bright, even contradictory, hues filled the space.

In addition, the whole ship was deluged with sound, the retail spaces pumping music and sound effects into the stillness of the ARK's main hall. Guerra even thought he heard a calliope spinning unsettling melodies into surrounding air.

Coulson clicked his teeth. "They really know how to set the mood, don't they?"

Guerra replied, "Either this is coincidental—an Act of God in the purest sense—or they know we're here."

"They know we're here," Sterling said quietly, peering up into the vast, illuminated expanse of the ship. "This is their version of a welcoming committee."

"The last place I went," Coulson shot back, "they tried to bribe us with chocolates and champagne."

Then, with a sigh, he added, "And prostitutes."

"Come on," Guerra said. "We've got ground to make up."

"Be on your toes," Katarina said. "Weapons charged, safeties on."

Pointing to the force gun in the kid's hands, Guerra asked, "You ready to use that thing?"

Sterling racked his weapon, causing it to hum with a charge cartridge. Coulson made a sound in the back of his throat to denote amusement.

Sterling ignored that.

"We have to make it to the main communications tower for the ship," he said. "If we make it there, we can call for back-up."

"And then?" Coulson asked.

"And then—we wait," Sterling replied. "Someone will be on the way soon after."

"How many people will die before that happens?" Guerra asked.

"Not enough," Coulson said. "If we have to wade through a sea of bodies to get there, I'm afraid to say some of y'all won't be going back. Plain and simple."

"I already said that," Sahana said.

"Well, I'm co-signing it," Coulson replied, "because I fucking believe it. We're doomed. Want me to spell it out? D-O-O—"

He was interrupted by the sound of a voice booming in through the loudspeakers above them.

THE ESSENCE OF OUR POWER IS IN THE STATE. FOR XENOGRAD, THE STATE IS ABSOLUTE. YOU MATTER, AND I MATTER, BUT WE ONLY REALLY MATTER IN CONNECTION TO OUR HOMELAND. WHAT ARE YOU DOING TODAY TO MAKE XENOGRAD BETTER?

"Propaganda much?" Coulson asked.

"That's the *Dear Leader*," said Sterling, his voice withering. "I would bet my life that we'll hear a whole lot more of this stuff before we're through."

Again, they reached the fork they had traversed before.

Sterling pressed a button on the side of his helmet to consult his briefing documents, projected in front of him in the form of a high definition hologram.

His eyes scanned the information with a rapidity and focus that impressed Guerra.

Maybe this kid *could* be a boon to their mission.

Guerra glanced over Sterling's shoulder as he perused the info—not that he could see anything. The UG had prototyped a technology that managed—somehow—to match specific documents to its owner. Something to do with a retinal scan, but Guerra didn't know.

Technology was not his strong suit.

What he *did* know was that no one else in the crew could see *his* briefing materials—and vice versa.

Oh, he could *open* Sterling's docs; he just couldn't *see* them. To his eye, they would be completely blank.

Which was a good thing—until the system broke down.

And perhaps that was what had happened, because Sterling's face twisted into a confused grimace.

"Where did it go?" he asked, speaking to no one in particular.

Guerra performed the same operation with his briefing materials and came up with a similar question. "Have the documents been erased, or is there some form of signal block coming from within the compound?"

"Let me think," he said.

Sterling turned and paced the square, using designated hand motions to run or restart the bureaucratic programs, while each member of the crew took inventory of various things.

Guerra made his way over to the statue, depicting a central figure —Dysart—flanked on either side by a rather severe-looking woman. The women were portrayed not as women but as human-shaped serpents.

Something about the look of it made him queasy, and not just for the grotesque imagery.

His mind turned it over.

If they could turn innocent people into raving, bloodthirsty monsters, couldn't the same be true of Dysart's familiars?

As Sterling paced, Sahana took up the space next to Guerra.

There was a fresh-looking addition on the broad side of the statue, done in bright orange spray paint.

JUSTICE TO BEATRIX.

Guerra raised one hand and ran his finger across the graffiti.

"There's that name again," he said.

Sahana nodded. "Maybe she's one of the girls. The, um—the *serpents*."

Guerra shook his head. "If Dysart was creating a political vacuum, no way was he sharing the spotlight with anyone."

"Touché," Sahana replied.

"Here," Guerra said, pointing at the plaque at the statue's base. "This language is different from my briefings. Instead of the Dear Leader, he's referred to as the 'Founder' and the two women as his 'Daughters of the Revolution.'"

Sahana nodded. "This ship is a petri dish for bad political ideas," she said, running one hand over the smooth surface of the Founder's feet. "And if the ideas are as new as these monuments, someone probably set fire to a powder keg."

"Seems likely."

"It frightens me to know what the people of this country endured to satisfy the political class. I look forward to performing my *duties* with the Xenograds, not subduing them in battle. I hope you understand that."

"I do, Sahana," Guerra replied. "This is an extreme situation, as well you know."

"I am a spiritual advisor," she said. "It is my duty to mend the wounds of political uncertainty and moral decay. I'm afraid it will be quite a long journey for many of this ship's inhabitants."

She paused, then said, "If there are any left."

The speaker above them crackled.

Another one of the announcements, only this one wasn't from the Dear Leader.

FEELING DOWN? INCAPABLE OF FINISHING STRONG ON YOUR SHIFT? HEY, NOT EVERYONE IS COMMITTED ENOUGH TO BE IN THE TRENCHES FOR SIXTEEN HOURS STRAIGHT! IF YOU FIND YOURSELF FEELING INFERIOR, STOP ON BY THE HEMLOCK & KEY FOR AN ENERGY BOOST! MODS FOR EVERY OCCASION. EVEN YOUR ANNIVERSARY, IF YOU KNOW WHAT I MEAN.

As the voice faded out, Sterling seemed to come out of his projection-induced coma.

"Okay, I think I got everything back online," he said finally. "If my docs are correct, we don't have to traverse the garden if we can move through the ARK National Museum."

Coulson—who had been sitting on a corner of the statue—immediately stood up.

"Hell yeah," he replied. "Let's do that."

"The only problem is," Sterling said, "if anything is locked or blocked, we'll have to circle back around, which will only make us more vulnerable."

Coulson held his torch-slash-weapon aloft. "I think we have that aspect of this little adventure covered, and I'll take that risk. If we have to detour, let's do that. The Founder's Garden is absolutely fucked."

Guerra glanced at Sahana, whose dark, almond-shaped eyes seemed full of mystery.

She wasn't easy to read, so Guerra breathed a sigh of relief when she nodded.

"Agreed," she said. "Let's go."

Sterling nodded and led the way.

∼

Very soon, they came to the end of the shopping promenade. The road grew dark again, the only light illuminating their path coming from fluorescents attached to the walls high above them.

"This is where it gets creepy again," Coulson said.

Guerra was unfazed. "Where does this lead?" he asked Sterling.

"If memory serves, we take a walk through this basic tenement building. Once we're above it and on the other side, we should be a few steps from the museum. We need only hoof it through that to get to the main communications station for the ARK."

"Great," Coulson said. "Let's do it."

He took a step forward, but Guerra stopped him.

"Listen," he said.

He didn't like what seemed to be coming from the other side of the promenade.

19

There was what sounded like a great gnashing of mechanical teeth—or something groaning under extreme weight.

Whatever it was, it was enormous—and it was on the ship. The only upside to its sudden appearance was that the...thing didn't seem to be nearby.

Once the jostling, clanging tumult faded, and the jangle of the promenade's bouncy rhythms returned, Guerra led them down the nearest path.

No one spoke for a long time, but when someone did, Guerra was surprised to find that it was Sterling.

"That was freaky," the kid said. "I wonder what it was."

"It doesn't say so in your little e-book?" Coulson asked.

"I don't know," Guerra replied, ignoring Coulson, "but I sincerely hope we get out of here before we run across it."

Coulson said, "A-fucking-men to that."

Guerra took stock of the rest of the group. Though she didn't say anything, Katarina clenched her jaw muscles taut. The ceremonial blue paint streaking her face gave her a dangerous look, and in thinking about the giant...*whatever* hiding out somewhere on the ship, Guerra was suddenly very comforted to have her around.

Sahana was calm as ever, but something in her face had changed. Her pursed lips had nearly disappeared, and her eyes had become sunken orbs, leaving dark shadows to play games with the contours of her face.

Guerra caught up to her as they walked.

"Your take on that...thing?"

Sahana shook her head. "It's just like you said. That is not something we want to encounter along this journey."

"Maybe that's what's giving you your, um, sense of foreboding about being here."

But Sahana on shook her head. "There are many reasons I feared stepping foot on the ARK, but that was not one of them."

"I bet it is now," Guerra replied, and she actually cracked a smile.

"Mostly what I have," she said, "is a grand sense of intuition. I pay close attention to what's around me. There's no magic in that—nothing...mystical."

"Right."

"But the part of my brain that is hyper sensitive to the vibrations of the universe tells me that, whatever that thing is, it is far worse than any quantity of the homicidal...displaced people on the ship."

Guerr replied, "I bet plenty of them are *locals*, too."

She nodded. "Perhaps I should have placed emphasis on a different word."

"Yeah—*homicidal*," Guerra replied.

He laughed, but she didn't. She smiled, but there was a chaste sense of duty to her gesture.

"At least we haven't seen any more of *them* since then," Guerra said, trying to change the subject.

Sahana frowned.

"What is it?"

"Well," she replied, "it's just that—well, what if we aren't seeing them because they were running from...that thing?"

Guerra felt all of his words freeze in his throat.

She had a point. And furthermore, was it possible that this world had gone insane because of the...*thing* lurking in the shadows of the ARK?

There was no evidence for that, and since he was a man of science, he had to live in that world, no matter how difficult it was not to speculate in every possible way about what was happening.

Dysart was likely experimenting on people he had transporting in, and those experiments had, somewhat ironically, resulted in the destruction of his little corner of the universe.

The sound—that was probably some malfunctioning piece of equipment on the ship, no?

He held close to that, even if the emotional part of him—the part that he drubbed mercilessly so that it would stay in the darkness—told him he was being ridiculous.

This part of him insisted they were being watched by a creature no human had seen before it ravaged the ARK, and that they were about to get an up close look at the thing.

"You okay?" Sahana asked him.

He turned to gaze at her. Sahana's long face had returned to its gentle former countenance, and so he relaxed.

A little.

"Yeah," he said. "I just—I can't help but think about the way my parents talked about the end of the world. This feels a lot like that, you know?"

Sahana seemed to understand what he was getting at. "There is real power in following the words and teachings of ancient books," she said, "but the real power is in our ability to interpret the world. That is where we bring forth the truth in our beliefs."

Guerra nodded. "I guess you're right."

She smiled enigmatically and said, "I sure hope so."

∽

THEY PASSED under a giant exit sign which read SHOPPING KEEPS YOU SAFE and worked quickly toward the tenement building's entrance. The whirly, unreal tinkling of the calliope kept the mood among them tense, but they could at least celebrate the fact that they had not encountered another murderous constituent of the ARK.

"You know," Sterling said, "this place is much cleaner than I thought it would be. Coming in, I expected a filthy, impoverished city. This is nothing of the sort. The streets are clean, and, outside of the looting, the shopping center was way less depressing than anticipated."

"Just wait," Guerra said. "We're in the public-facing arena. This is probably where past dignitaries have been taken. Its purpose is to put visitors at ease. Once we get into the depths of the ARK, if it's still clean and well-kept, then you can be impressed."

Down the road a ways, blocking their path was a security checkpoint. It was something you'd expect to see in a place like this, and though it was abandoned, it had an ominous look about it.

They approached and stopped when a light just above the body scanner flashed red.

"Normally, there'd be soldiers here to inspect us and turn us back or let us through," Guerra said. "Looks like security has abandoned its post."

"Just like everything else out here," Sahana said, her eyes gazing into the distance.

The place was set up like an old-fashioned car checkpoint, but in place of the striped bar going across the pathway, there was a high fence gate. Coulson took another step forward, and an alarm sounded. Three short, low-pitched barks from the speakers above them.

"Warning," a voice from the speakers said. "Step back and wait to be ushered through the checkpoint."

They waited a moment, but of course no one appeared.

"Fuck this," Coulson said, at last, and then he was trudging toward the gate, force gun in tow.

The alarm emitted a triplicate of beeps, and the red light flashed, just before a previously unseen rifle appeared. The air cracked, and the ground at Katarina's feet exploded in a spray of faux-marble. The bullet ricocheted and clanged off into the distance.

"Holy shit!" Coulson screamed as he dove to one side.

Katarina took a step forward. She raised her sub-auto machine gun and fired a burst. The red light flickered and died, just as the whirring sound beneath it wound down.

After that, she turned her attention to the ceiling-mounted weapon and took it out with a well-placed burst of gunfire. The gate clicked, caught, and then slid open with nary a hitch.

"Let's go," Katarina said, slinging her gun over her shoulder as she strolled through the gate.

"See, I told you it was fine," Coulson said, smiling sheepishly.

They all followed.

As they crossed the checkpoint threshold, Katarina stopped and then bade them stop, as well. A simple wave of the hand from the war-hardened warrior, and they became instant statues.

"You hear something?"

Normally, they might have been supplied with very fine (and very expensive) equipment to measure their surroundings. Night-vision goggles and all sorts of technology. Because this was a diplomatic mission, they had been deprived of all that.

"We're not alone," she said. "Prepare yourselves."

And then the next moment, the first of *them* appeared.

"Here we go," said Katarina.

She sounded excited to be back in danger.

If that's the case, he thought, you got your wish.

20

The first thing Guerra noticed was that the approaching figure *looked* human. Two feet, two arms, and a head. In any other city in any other ship on any other day, he might have staggered right past without a second look.

A bum looking for a drink.

A mentally ill beggar, pleading for help.

It made Guerra wonder just how many infected people had wandered by one another as this...plague began to get its hooks into them.

The figure stumbled toward them, standing and moving, despite the fact that its motions were both inexplicable and inhuman. It was an abomination, and yet it existed.

This thing—it looked like an upright spider. Arms and legs bent at odd angles as it perambulated forward, the twitchy, monstrous gestures indicating the sickness was not simply physical or mental, but a precise combination of both.

The fact that most of its movements were obscured by shadow did not make it any less frightening.

"Wait for it," Guerra said. "Let's see what he does."

It was a silly request, because Guerra knew Katarina wouldn't take orders from anyone who wasn't Katarina.

Once the figure appeared in the light, the crew got a fantastic look at what ravages had been visited upon it.

The skin not covered in clothing had been torn off or otherwise worn away. At first, Guerra thought it was a man, but at this close range he couldn't be sure. It looked like a textbook's anatomical drawing of a person. There was blood and sinew and tendons but little else.

The eyes—as blue as the oceans Guerra had only seen on computer screens—conveyed humanity, but everything else was blood and bone. What flesh remained hung in withered and grayed wings from the shoulders. It was as though the creature was shrugging off a snug sweatshirt and had given up halfway through.

The white specks that covered the red, ghastly monstrosity began to wriggle and fall off, and when the thing shuffled a few more steps forward, they could see that the specks were, indeed, maggots. The milky white fly larvae writhed and crawled, moving into and out of the body's crevasses.

Then, just as Guerra was beginning to get a visual handle on the creature before them, *it* saw them.

"What do we do?" Coulson whispered, and Guerra held up a placating hand.

"Hold tight," he said. "I want to see the reaction."

The lolling, absurd eyeballs landed on Guerra, specifically, and then things began to move quickly toward their end. The walking figure tilted its head to one side and stopped on the street corner.

Just as abruptly, it screamed and charged.

Guerra readied himself to give an order, but he was a half-beat too late.

A single shot from Katarina's rifle took it down.

The lopsided, barely human figure toppled forward, being carried by momentum, and lay screaming in its own filth and waste.

Incoherent, inhuman syllables emerged from the figure's lipless mouth as they approached, as if the unhinged raving might actually conjure a fourth-dimensional demon of some sort.

And then Guerra thought about the impossibly large creature lumbering around somewhere in the ship's depths, and suddenly that thought wasn't so funny.

As they stood over it, the figure tried—and failed—to get up, but the ranting continued.

And then, all at once, it stopped. The creature allowed its skinless cranium to drop freely to the ground, and then it seemed to sigh.

"Any last words?" Coulson asked, and the thing—in defiance of all logic and physics—managed a smile.

"Blood—and soil," it managed, and then the creature expired.

The scene was silent, save for the sickening *urp—urp—urp* of the maggots making dinner out of their host.

"The fuck is blood and soil?" Coulson asked at last.

"It was a Nazi thing," Sterling said, half-convincingly. "I think it had something to do with racial purity."

Coulson glanced from the kid to Guerra, who shrugged.

"I got no idea," he said, "but yeah—it sounds about right."

Coulson said, "But I thought these fucking things were supposed to be the ship's poor, huddled masses, yearning to breathe free and all that shit."

"That wasn't one of the refugees," Sahana said. "He—or she—is a native Xenogradian."

"So this isn't just a disease among the wretched refuse of the ARK, then," Coulson said.

"It appears that way," Guerra acquiesced. "But there's only really one way to figure out. Watch my six."

Guerra knelt next to the figure and then rummaged around in his pack until he found a pair of sanitary gloves.

Coulson said, "Please tell me you're not going to—oh, god, you're actually doing it."

Guerra peeled what remained of the lips aside and peeked inside the mouth. He then did another cursory examination and sat down on his haunches, inspecting the figure.

"It's bleeding from the eyes and the gums," Guerra said.

"Yeah, no shit," Coulson said. "She—or he or it—was bleeding from everywhere else. Why *not* the gums?"

"What's that mean?" Katarina asked.

Guerra shrugged, looking up at the group. "Malaria. Ebola. Could be any number of filoviruses."

Sterling gasped. "Which would mean we're all infected. It's spread through blood, right? We've all been sprayed with blood mist."

"Don't panic," Guerra said. "We don't have any indication a filovirus is what it is. And if it is—well, then, we'll deal with it when it becomes serious."

"I consider all of this *very* serious," Sterling said.

But Guerra ignored him.

He then pulled an all-purpose knife from his pack and felt along the decedent's stomach until he seemed content. Then, he sliced open the abdomen and reached three fingers inside.

"That's a lot of blood," he said. "There's not enough skin to be certain, but I think the body was hemorrhaging between the skin and the muscles."

"What's that mean?"

"Something very bad," Guerra said.

"So it's a fucking outbreak of Ebola on this ship?" Coulson said. "And we're digging around in this thing's body?"

Sterling said, "Wait, what's the death rate for Ebola?"

"Oh, about ninety percent."

Coulson rolled his eyes. "Jesus Christ. Just my luck. I could have been doing security on one of the ships that specializes in hospitality. You know that? Fake beaches and little drinks with the umbrellas and courtesans. The whole thing."

Then, Guerra flipped the body over.

"What are you doing now?" Sterling asked.

"The colon's full of blood," Guerra replied. "He or she or it has been sloughing off parts of intestine like dead skin cells. It's not a confirmation of this being a filovirus, but it's damn close."

Sterling smacked his helmet. "Oh, God. I don't—I don't think I can handle this. I—I'm freaking out."

He was hyperventilating, and it seemed like he might actually faint. He leaned against the nearest wall and slid down until he bumped the ground.

Guerra gently removed his gloves and tossed them onto the body. From his pack, he removed a small bottle of industrial cleaner and scrubbed his suit up to the elbows.

Meanwhile, the group's attention never quite left the pitiable image of the face-down figure.

Sahana finally broke the silence. She said, "This isn't a virus. At least not in the way you're saying it is. It is contagious, but you're not going to contract it through handling the body."

"That's the logical explanation," Guerra said.

"Maybe the logical answer isn't correct, in this situation," Sahana replied.

"It's a filovirus," Guerra finished. "Or maybe you're just engaging in magical thinking. In *hoping* it's not the outcome you're want. You should resist that thinking."

Sahana's posture changed then. She stood up straight, jaw set, and said, "Tell me something about *your* thinking on this."

"Fair enough."

"You have been in situations where a filovirus was present, yes?"

Guerra nodded. "Two years ago. I was sent in as an envoy to observe and report on an outbreak in a ship. A woman died while giving birth to a stillborn baby. They were both infected."

"What else?"

"The priest who administered last rites wiped the dead woman's bloody tears from her face, and then he used the same cloth to dry his own eyes."

"So he was infected?"

Guerra nodded. "From there, the disease spread like wildfire across the ship. This priest, he administered to dozens of families in the days after his infection."

Sahana smiled bitterly. "Did the priest go on a murderous rampage after he was infected?"

The group's eyes ping-ponged between the two, and Guerra felt them all glaring at him.

His smile was a logical counter to her own. "I think you and I both know the answer to that," he said. "He became ill, and he began to vomit. Black vomit. Had what looked like coffee grounds in it. That was partially digested portions of his stomach lining."

"And *then*," Sahana asked, "did he begin to attack and rip apart his fellow villagers?"

"No," Guerra responded curtly. "He began to hemorrhage giant portions of his intestines out of his rectum. It sloughed off like petals from a dying flower, and then he died."

His face grew hot with shame and embarrassment, and he knew he should have resisted his desire to bloviate about past missions.

With his embarrassment, the old insecurities returned. He only *thought* he was a leader. He didn't feel it, didn't think he could command the attention or the respect of people like Katarina or Coulson—especially if Sahana could see right through him.

So he sat back and let himself get flayed for his mistake.

"I have seen Ebola, *too*, Guerra," she said. "It does not turn you into a superhuman soldier of murder. It shuts your body down slowly over several days, and you die a horrible death. But at no point are you leaping onto spaceships and trying to tear through the walls."

The mystic let that sink in.

"Just because you know *something*, peace officer," Sahana continued, "does not mean that you know *everything*."

"I hear you," Guerra said, but his apology was overshadowed by Katarina snapping her fingers at them.

"Hurry," said Katarina, "I hear more of our comrades approaching. They're on their way."

With that, the rest of the group began to move toward the tenement building.

"You're right," Guerra said, as they walked away. "I was wrong. I jumped to the wrong conclusion and didn't think things through before I came to that conclusion."

The group nodded, and it was apparent by their faces he'd taken it much more seriously than *they* had.

He added, "But let's not kid ourselves about what's happening to these people. It's unnatural, and it's transmittable. That should make us all very afraid."

"We can argue later," Coulson said. "If we get the hell out of here in a hurry, we won't have to worry about catching whatever the fuck this is."

As the tunnel darkened ahead of them, a new group of spidery, insectoid enemies appeared in the distance.

Katarina waited until they had lumbered into view, and then she raised her rifle and downed them with a few quick bursts. Her expression remained as docile and calm as ever as she did so.

"If you get them in the head," she said, "they go down much faster. Just keep that in mind."

"I don't even feel like I'll need to carry my weapon," Coulson said.

"Yes, but you *will*," Katarina said, and then she was moving forward.

21

The Rohm Tenements appeared, on first glance, as stylishly built apartments for Xenograd's less fortunate citizens, but the moment one entered them, it became apparent that they were made more for livestock than human beings.

Just walking through them produced an uncomfortable feeling.

They were cramped, dirty, and foul-smelling, not to mention the fact that due to they were completely uninhabitable.

Like they had been constructed in a hurry. Or like the builders didn't care about the people inhabiting them.

Rats openly defied the presence of human beings, standing on their hind legs and hissing as if their territory had been usurped. Cockroaches scaled the walls in numbers that caused Guerra too shiver.

"It makes me itchy just fucking *being* in here," Coulson said. "This place would be better served if I used my torch to burn it all down."

"This is the lowest level of human existence on the ARK," Guerra said. "One of two things is true: they were built poorly to house a group the ruling class didn't care about, or they were built quickly because they didn't expect a large influx of immigrants."

"Either way," Sahana said, "this is inhuman."

Guerra said, "When you see people as things that can either serve you or grant you power, you stop worrying about the little things—like common decency."

"It's one of the greatest and most obvious failings of totalitarian governments," Sterling added. "They often boast that a classless society is best, but social stratification happens everywhere. Even in a place where the wealth is 'shared.'"

The elevator was not functioning, and the stairwell had been destroyed, in parts, so the crew had to ascend by means of a kind of measured climbing, in which they traversed a bunch of rubble and garbage to reach the next working set of stairs.

"Thank god we're wearing masks," Coulson said, "or else I'd probably be tossing my cookies everywhere. I have this—thing. I can handle some pretty foul shit. But when I see people this fucking poor—it just sickens me."

Guerra rolled his eyes. "I'm sure these people would appreciate your compassion."

"Serve and protect," Coulson replied, offering a mock salute in return.

The rooms reeked of filth, and laid on top was the stench of death. It was like wandering into a wrecked funeral parlor, and it got worse with each passing step.

Their masks—outfitted with complex air filters—managed to vacuum away some of the smell.

But only some.

There was garbage everywhere. Long forgotten bags of used diapers and rotten food, left out like bodies after a bloody war on contested ground.

Oh, and there were bodies, too. Those which had not completely decomposed lay in hallways, struck down by weapons or sickness, and at this point, it didn't much matter how. They were dead, and they had been left to rot.

Occasionally, one of them would accidentally step into the *middle* of a body, some kind of sludgy, gelatinous mixture of bone and flesh, and let out an awful, surprised gasp, one that would send them fumbling for the safeties on their weapons.

Only Katarina seemed unmoved by it all. She traversed the space without the standard complaints offered by her counterparts in the UG.

"How are you able to stand the intensity of this *stench*?" Sterling asked at one point.

Katarina shrugged. "I've been in worse."

"Don't you know," Coulson said," that Katarina vacations in Hell? It's a nice break from her normal, everyday life. Shit, *this* is a walk in the park. Am I wrong, Kat?"

But Katarina didn't respond. Guerra had observed, for the most part, Katarina only spoke when she felt the need to, or if it benefited the entire group.

This was not one of those times.

Guerra was no expert on his crew, but prior to taking this mission, he had read up on Katarina Hashimoto's troubled—and yet, decorated—past. There was plenty to unpack about her, and besides, his superiors had warned him about her.

"She is an excellent soldier," Frank Marcello had told him. "Highly intelligent. Respectful. Quiet. *Discreet*."

"Then what's the problem?"

Marcello had given a look that might resemble shame in someone who had not witnessed the kind of unencumbered evil he had.

He had told Guerra in so many words that she was due for a freakout. Her test scores related to battle trauma had been ticking up ever slightly in the last year, and every mission had led her closer to what the old guys might call *shell-shock*.

"Then why are you sending her on *this* one?" he'd asked.

"You have to do what you have to do," Marcello had said. "It is imperative to keep the galaxy safe, and when that happens, you have to take some chances. That's why *you* are top dog on this, too, my friend."

And so that had been that.

Katarina was on the mission, and thank everything holy for that. She had been amazing thus far.

But it was, of course, necessary for him to take the initiative to check into her past himself, since Katarina was no more likely to delineate the details of her past than she was to climb onto a bar and sing karaoke.

She had been born the child of two renowned scientists, whom Guerra suspected had been contracted to work in the weapons labs for their home country.

When Katarina was just fourteen, her parents disappeared. Given the fact that they lived on a ship floating in a sea of darkness, it was unlikely they just up and changed identities. However, there was a fair amount of speculation about the subject, and though Guerra was unable to read all of the redacted documents, he was able to gather some context about the disappearance.

They had been working on a top secret project, though the details of that work were, of course, lost to time (or a digital shredder). It required the utmost secrecy and highest credentials. When their room was found covered in blood, everyone suspected foul play.

When the bodies never turned up, it became one of her home ship's most contentious mysteries. After months of searching, the police department labeled the scene a homicide and closed the case.

It only got stranger from there.

A cloud lingered just above Katarina's head for most of her young life, and she did nothing to bat away the surrounding funk. She continued to receive good grades, and when she failed in life, she persevered, but there was always the question of her involvement in her parents' deaths.

The first and most obvious question people asked about Katarina Hashimoto was, "Why in the world would she have anything at all to do with her parents' disappearance?"

Most people would not be wrong for thinking it was too tawdry a tale to connect with a fourteen-year-old. The Hashimotos were professionals with ties to deep pocketed members of the government, and for the length of the first investigation, it was believed someone with a sizable amount of money and *beaucoup* influence had "disappeared" the doting parents.

But as the investigative unit dug deeper into the histories of both parents and saw nothing but the utmost respect and transparency from subordinates, bosses, and other coworkers, they were drawn to a single detail that seemed to unsettle one particular member of the unit.

Because Katarina was both young and a seeming victim in this tragedy, her alibi was not questioned—early on. Not only that, for the first year, no one even seemed to care *where* she had been on the night of her parents' disappearance. When she'd said "out with friends," people believed her, and that was that. As the investigation dried up and produced no new leads, however, one of the homicide investigators—a man named Hakurai—circled back around to restart the search from the ground up.

What he found in Katarina Hashimoto was not a delicate victim but a cagey, withdrawn teenager, someone who did not seem to know the answers to the very basic questions she was being asked. According to the investigating officer investigating, it wasn't as though she'd forgotten her alibi because of the passage of time; it was because she'd never cared to come up with an excuse in the first place.

By then, any evidence of an actual crime had completely disappeared. Shortly after Katarina's second interview with the authorities, two men with lengthy rap sheets ended up disemboweled in a bad part of town.

She went on to become a veteran of foreign wars, going to the front lines in any and all engagements with hostile adversaries, to the point that she had a complete mental breakdown in the middle of a firefight some six or seven years after joining. Just…sat right down in the middle of a war zone.

After rehab—code for *mental institution*—she returned to her position, but she was never the same. Didn't talk much, but she nevertheless continued her military career.

It was not coincidental that she worked with intelligence services, and soon after found herself at the UG. It was rumored her home country didn't quite know what else to do with her that was legal, but then again, that portion of her file was redacted, so Guerra could only guess.

So when Guerra found himself walking next to Katarina in the tenement building, her clenching her gun a little too tightly, it was all the research he'd digested over the previous weeks that was at the forefront of his mind.

"This place—it's a shithole," she said.

So far, Xenograd was nothing more than yet another tortured example of a failed state. Something people at the UG had seen more times than could reliably be counted.

But Guerra could tell the soldier wanted to say something. It was very rare for her to communicate anything that wasn't a cold, hard fact, so this was uncharted territory.

He waited, wondering what might be on her mind.

In the end, though, she closed her mouth and stared emotionlessly at a fixed point in the distance.

"Are we making a mistake?" Guerra asked. "Do we need to turn tail and go back the way we came?"

When she didn't answer, Guerra spoke again. "I trust you. You and I both know I do. I'm just the mouthpiece for this trip. I talk—it's all I do. You *lead* us. And if you tell me we are doing this mission a disservice—"

"I know the way," she said. "We have some rubble to traverse, but that will be no real problem for us. Just follow close and keep your eyes open for more of...them."

"They bother you, don't they?"

She shook her head. "No more than any other thing does."

"Then what is it?"

He'd tried to time his response so that he could catch her off-guard, that he could find a way to break through the armor, but she was prepared.

She was always prepared.

"All this dust is going to play hell on my weapon," she said, and then she stepped forward, moving through a long hallway, headed for the opposite stairwell.

Oh, well, he thought. At least I tried.

He hoped she would open up, if the need arose.

They passed yet another dead body. This one was crawling with maggots, no different than the one back near the building's entrance.

Sahana cleared her throat.

"If this is where a great number of the people in this ship lived," Sahana said, "then what does the rest of the ship consist of? What's waiting for us at the top?"

"Let's hope we don't have to go to the top of this monstrosity," Guerra said. "Sterling says the comms station is on the other side of this apartment building. We can call the cavalry to come and save us from ourselves."

"Let's hope," was Sahana's quiet reply.

All throughout the building, there were posters both lionizing the Dear Leader and warning against the ship's perceived enemies. Most of them depicted Dysart as a larger-than-life hero, but there was also an undercurrent of distrust for another, not specifically named group, as well.

One poster read, *The Founder is the way and the light. The Stowaway lives in darkness and shadow.*

"Maybe there is something to the idea that the country had issues with outsiders," Sterling said.

Guerra thought the claim was dubious. "It's a common tactic for undemocratic rulers to turn the people against one another. If they believe themselves to be unfairly maligned by some other group, they'll support the boss, no matter what."

"Still," Sterling said, "this looks pretty specific. What do you think it's about?"

They kept walking, and they continued to come across various pieces of propaganda, all warning the people of the ARK about a blue-eyed, dark-skinned group, never actually named but deemed to be vile, nonetheless.

The posters exaggerated their blue eyes and their large mouths, and they were very often depicted with the face of a human and the body of a snake, slithering across the poster in a devious manner.

"What nationality is that?" Sterling asked. "Who are these people?"

Guerra shrugged. "Political uprising? Maybe the proletariat had enough of *Herr Dysart* and started an information war against him."

Just then, Guerra heard a *thump*, and it wasn't just faulty construction coming to settle in this giant coffin of a ship.

The next moment, a sagging, water-logged wall exploded inward, and a horde of *them* appeared in its wake.

Guerra didn't hesitate.

"Run!" he shouted into his headset, and the crew responded in earnest, sprinting down the hallway to some indeterminate point, some future haven where they could hide.

"Pay attention to what's ahead of you," Guerra said, much as he didn't really believe it. "What you don't see might represent your end as much as what's behind you."

Coulson said, "Easy for you to say, chief. You must be too hearing impaired to get a sense of what the fuck is chasing us."

The attackers—don't call them zombies, he thought—were gaining on them, and even though Guerra was confident there was a light at the end of this tunnel somewhere, he didn't know that he could see it quite yet.

They reached a stairwell and continued up, the sound of their feet thumping on the stairs the only sound besides the raving screams of their pursuers and their own breathy exhalations.

"I didn't fucking train for this," Coulson said at some point.

"None of us did," Katarina replied, and that was pretty much that.

Every so often, the soldier—who was at the back of their little formation—would stop, turn, and fire down the stairs at the screaming multitude, not really taking them out but momentarily slowing them down so the crew could make up some ground.

Guerra himself felt a loosening of his hold on the situation. What would he tell them if they became overrun?

Save yourselves?

Stand and fight?

Would he have the courage to stay behind and fight, letting them continue on while he himself was devoured by this throng of hungry, insane monsters?

At last, the situation broke, and they managed to hit some good fortune.

They reached the outermost exit at the top of the tenement building. It was the only visible exit, and so Guerra didn't think that there was going to be a flood of those...things coming after them from somewhere else.

At least not yet.

But even though the exit door locked behind them, there was no way to secure it against the sheer force of the beasts.

"If we don't close it down," Guerra said, "they'll be right along on our heels."

What he didn't add but wanted to was, *and that will be the end of us.*

Coulson, thinking quickly on his feet, said, "Let's use that!"

Beside them was a statue of none other than Generalissimo Dysart, one hand held high in the air in salute, not unlike a famed and terrible authoritarian back on Earth.

They all got situated behind the fallen statute and began to push, each using every bit of strength provided to them.

But it did nothing.

They tried again, their sad grunts only seeming to indicate that they were absolutely, totally doomed.

"It's not *moving!*" Guerra said.

He could feel his grip going, his hands sweaty and ineffectual at this work.

Sahana made eye contact with him and said, "Believe it will. Believe it will."

But all Guerra could focus on was just how little effect their actions were having on it. If faith were a muscle you could work, his had withered away on the bone.

Guerra's lack of faith—shriveled though it was—was not the deciding factor here.

It was the strength of his crew mates, who managed to tear the statue from its mooring and thrust it in front of the exit, just as the beings on the other side reached the top landing.

The things slammed against the door. They fanned out and lunged against the walls, too.

Guerra checked his surroundings. The building was structurally sound, but he didn't know that the architects and builders had rated it for—

(*don't say zombie*)

—zombie attacks. So he wasn't sure how long it would hold out against this kind of onslaught.

Then, a telltale crack appeared in the building's wall, and much to his (and the rest of the crew's) chagrin, it threatened to break.

They turned and fled in the opposite direction, not slowing down until they reached a point where they could not hear the beasts screaming.

"Did you *believe* enough?" Coulson asked.

"I guess so," Guerra replied, though he was too shellshocked to know one way or the other.

"The question I have," Sterling added, "is where are the rest of them?"

22

They did not travel even the length of a good-sized soccer field before the smell wafted out to them.

"I think we found the rest of the dead bodies," Sterling said.

They had followed a path down from the tenement building to a small theater, and as they stood in its looming shadow, the smell almost overpowered them.

"Well," Coulson asked, looking around, "where are they?"

Sterling, using his hand to flip through several screens on his display, turned ninety degrees to his right and pointed.

"If my—admittedly outdated—map is correct," Sterling said, "then we can take the path through this theater and end up on the far end of the next level up on the ship."

Coulson asked, "And how close to the comms signal will we be?"

"Close," Sterling said.

"Are you sure?"

The kid glanced from Guerra to Coulson. He looked through his display once more and then shook his head.

"No," he said. "I have no fucking idea."

Coulson barked with laughter.

"I hope your parents are rich enough to buy me off," Coulson said, "because I am blackmailing the *shit* out of them after we get out of this."

∼

THE THEATER WAS CALLED The Grand Guignol, and they followed Coulson through its elaborate front doors.

What they found in place of the working theater was something of a bizarre *tableau vivant*.

"Fucking hell," Coulson said, whistling. "That's got to be at least five hundred people."

The theater's seating was packed with people, each of them dead and facing the stage.

"This could be a trap," Sterling said. "One of the profiles of Xenograd I read relayed a story about a massacre Dysart perpetrated on his way to becoming president."

"What happened?" Guerra asked, inspecting one of the corpses lounging in his permanent seat.

Guerra himself didn't even know about it. He'd read the prep documents backward and forward and hadn't seen anything about a massacre like this.

And then a troubling thought occurred to him.

Was the kid lying?

Followed, of course, by another thought that betrayed his prejudices against the rich kid.

Or had his daddy's organization granted him access to even *more* private documents, ones even the United Galaxy didn't know about?

Neither was a good prospect, and so he hoped neither was true.

Sterling said, "Dysart invited a political rival to dinner, only to close off and gas the whole building before the main course was served."

"Fuck," Coulson said. "That's brutal. I mean—no steak? No chicken? Just *appetizers*?"

Sahana gave the medic a withering look

"Well," Guerra said, ignoring Coulson, "this isn't a stretch from situation, since it's closed off and everyone is dead."

The kid looked up from his inspection of a woman, whose face was covered with a canvas bag.

"Then the theater really lives up to the name," he said, his voice barely above a whisper.

"The fuck does that mean?"

Sahan elbowed Coulson, who glanced angrily at him. "What?"

"*Grand Guignol*?" Sterling said, looking from group member to group member. "The name of the theater?"

"You're not talking fast," Coulson said, "but I'm going to need you to slow down for me."

"It's a play on the old French theater type. Grand Guignol shows."

Guerra shrugged. "You keep saying that word—"

"They were plays performed in the Pigalle district of Paris, and the main feature was extreme, realistic violence."

"And so that's what Grand Guignol means?"

"Well, no," Sterling replied. "It means 'Theater of the Great Puppet.' But that's the point."

"What *is* the point?"

Sterling took this opportunity to take a stroll down the main aisle, his eyes on the dead victims.

"The point," Sterling said, "is that this is a production. Instead of being on the stage, however, it's out here in the audience. This violence, it's real, and it's also a *play*. It's meant to say something."

"Yeah," Coulson replied, "how fucking sick the guy who did it is. That's what it says to me."

Sterling knelt down next to the nearest dead and inspected it. "They've all been tied to their chairs."

He used his thumb and forefinger to pinch the twine that held the decedent's wrist to the armrest.

"What's that on their heads?" Coulson asked.

"Cloth sack," he replied. "There are eyeholes cut in each one, but they're tied at the neck."

The specimen Sterling was inspecting was a woman of indeterminate age.

She had been dead a long time.

Her body had been mostly preserved, but the skin was a brittle, paper thin quality.

That's not what was alarming.

No, what drew the eye to the woman was the bright purple color of the flesh on the neck. It was like one giant bruise—consistent with ligatures used in strangulation—and yet it was a deeper color than any bruises Guerra had ever seen.

"And what's in the sack?"

The kid shrugged. "Maybe for the effect? I mean, there *are* eyeholes here."

Sterling carefully untied the strings that bound the sack.

The next moment, there was a sound and a scream, and it all seemed to happen at once.

"Jesus Fucking Christ!"

A creature dropped heavily from the head-sack. Sterling leaped backward.

"It's a fucking snake!"

The rest of the crew backed up. Even Katarina took a cautious step away from the scene.

All of them receded to the rear of the theater except Sahana, who knelt in the aisle and crept closer to where they had last seen the slithering reptile.

With a quick snap of the hand, she plucked the creature from its place among the expired audience members and held it aloft.

The snake was smooth gray with a white underbelly. Two black eyes punctuated what was otherwise an unremarkable face. It was a long beast of a thing, too, over ten feet in length.

"What is it?" Sterling asked. "I mean, what kind?"

"*Dendroaspis polylepis*," she said.

"The fuck does that mean?" Coulson asked.

Sahana almost smiled, but not quite. She twisted the animal's jaw slightly, and the creature's mouth opened wide.

The inside was as black as charcoal.

"Black mamba," she said. "And an ornery one, too."

Sterling opened his mouth to speak but then readjusted himself and asked a more meaningful one.

"*How* lethal is it?"

"Oh, some say the *most* lethal," she replied. "And they're quick, too. You wouldn't want to be caught in a corner with one."

She looked as comfortable with the reptile as she did with just about anything else. She was calm but firm and kept her attention on what lay in front of her.

Which, in this case, was a deadly, dangerous snake.

"One bite," Sahana continued, "and you'd be on your back within the hour."

Sterling took a conscious step backward.

"You'd have a little while contending with the pain, and then you'd slide into respiratory failure. After that, your heart would go, and that would be that."

"Is that what happened here?" Guerra asked.

Coulson waved one hand around. "They all have the sack cloth on their heads. What do *you* think?"

Guerra shook his head. "It just seems like an oddly elaborate punishment to level on a whole auditorium's worth of people. Why would they do that to someone?"

The diplomat looked out over the deceased crowd and imagined how much work—how much *planning*—it must have taken to organize such a grisly scene of horror.

And for what?

Sahana said, "If I ventured to guess, I'd say this was meant to make a statement."

"A political one?"

She considered it. "Possibly," she said. "The eyes are cut out of a number of the sacks, which meant that they were supposed to die witnessing something."

"That's what *I* was saying," Sterling said, optimistically. It must have been exciting to be validated, Guerra thought.

Coulson looked dubious. "How the fuck did you get all of that from one little peek at these people's masks?"

Sahana stared him down and said, "Why don't you stalk your ass up to the stage and take a peek? Save us some trouble?"

The medic looked from the mystic to the stage and then back again, his expression never changing from the self-satisfied smirk that almost always seemed to grace his expression.

"The question is," Sterling said, standing up and facing the stage, "what were they being forced to watch?"

The rest of them, including Coulson, followed his gaze. The stage curtains were closed, and the effect was ominous.

"Only one way to find out," Sahana said, trudging down the center aisle.

Guerra watched her go, feeling very much like it should have been *him* to take this chance. It was *his* crew, so he believed it was *his* responsibility.

Once Sahana reached the end of the aisle, she stopped.

"You ready for this?"

When she pulled the curtains aside, the whole of the scene was revealed, and suddenly, it all made sense.

At center stage, a white, three tier podium had been set up, and on each tier was a giant brown sack, not unlike the ones covering the spectators' heads.

Blood seeped down the front of each tier, pooling on the stage's hardwood floor.

"It's safe to come up," Sahana said, and they did just that.

Coulson clicked his teeth. "I'm fucking terrified to know what might be in each one of those bags."

They stood in front of the podium in silence for a minute before Coulson sighed.

"Well," he said, "let's get to it."

And they did.

Coulson knelt in front of the topmost bag and used a two-sided blade to cut the end off.

"Ready yourselves," he said.

He traveled around back and grabbed the burlap by the closed end and pulled.

It was worse than Guerra could have imagined.

Blood and gore of all sorts slipped free of the sack, thudding to the ground at the crew's feet as they groaned in disgust and horror.

It was an abomination of butchery. Human viscera and dismembered body parts had been mixed with what looked like animal carcasses.

The other contents were not immediately recognizable, but that didn't prevent Katarina from taking full inventory of it all.

She glowered at the mess of body parts and blood for a moment before ticking them off on her fingers.

"Looks like a snake—"

"Expected," Coulson said.

"A monkey, a dog, and—of course—a human being."

Sterling turned a queasy shade of green but managed to chew back whatever was threatening to come up.

"This—this is an ancient punishment," he said, once he was back to normal. "The Romans purportedly used to do this to people who committed patricide."

"And that's true?"

Sterling shook his head. "It was probably more rare than the histories would suggest."

Coulson grimaced. "Whose fucking dad did these pieces of shit kill?"

Sterling almost rolled his eyes. "It's a metaphor. If I had to guess, I'd say these three were the main culprits, and they managed to convert about five hundred people to their cause of overthrowing the government."

"Then what about patricide?"

"Well, in an autocracy," Guerra said, "the leader *is* the father. Hence, this little exercise in defiance was seen as a slight against the *family* on the ship. Not just Dysart himself."

Guerra thought about it all, the weight of his contemplations dragging his mind down into darkness.

"What does that *out there*"—meaning those ravenous things chasing them through Xenograd—"have to do with this *in here*?"

But Sterling could only shrug. "No idea," he said. "Everything I know comes from the documents I was given."

"Sahana?"

She met eyes with Guerra, but she, too, could come up with nothing. "Unless the coup itself is *because* of what's happening outside."

Guerra considered it. "Or maybe it has something to do with Beatrix?"

"The fuck is *Beatrix*?" Coulson asked.

"The girl—the *name* on the statues," Guerra said, keeping his voice under control. Coulson was really getting on his nerves. "If people are spray-painting her name on monuments to Dysart, then there has to be a reason, right?"

It occurred to him that this Beatrix could be one of the poor bastards in the sacks. Or one of the many unfortunate souls tied to a chair out in the theater.

A dream deferred, he thought.

Dysart *must* have been paranoid to engage in this kind of performative authoritarianism, with the world crumbling around him the way it was.

And then he encountered a rogue thought, one that seemed to come out of nowhere and bash him across the cheek.

Or maybe she is no one at all. A phantom created by the opposition to sew discord among the Xenograd's many inhabitants.

But this wasn't discord.

It didn't feel like it, anyway.

No, this wasn't a coup, a revolution. This was a funeral procession, a floating coffin, with the wild dogs out in the streets, fighting over the scraps.

The thought chilled him to his bones.

"Hold on a second," Sterling said. "Over here, there's a switch. It seems to be attached to the projection system."

"No," Guerra said. "That might alert the—"

But it was already too late. Sterling had already flipped the switch, and the screen was coming down.

An ancient projector on the ceiling rattled to life, sending a blinding white light in their direction.

The crew fumbled down from the stage and peered up at this new revelation with some—but not total—interest.

Until the video's subject appeared on-screen.

General Commander Dysart grinned from behind a desk like a doctor offering up a positive prognosis.

He wagged one finger at the camera and said,

"I have something to confess to you, and I don't know that you will like it. But here goes."

And the crew held its collective breath for the authoritarian's confession.

23

Dysart was a short man, slender and sharp-featured, like he had been carved economically from a small piece of stone. Above his lip was a razor thin mustache and below his cavernous brow were two eyes darkened by shadow. They practically seemed to float in the center of his head.

He wore the typical military garb of a banana republic's leader, but there was something different about this man. Something Guerra couldn't quite figure out just yet.

"Maybe he'll admit that he's pranking the incoming UG officials by pretending that his ship has been taken over by bloodthirsty monsters."

"Wishful thinking," Guerra said, but his attention was fixed on the screen.

He was hoping to get some insight from the leader's statement, even if these kinds of addresses were usually ninety percent bullshit.

Guerra was good at face-to-face statesmanship. He had studied under the tutelage of Truman Li—rest his soul—and was willing to take risks, when he knew what the proper outcome of a diplomatic voyage was supposed to be.

He never imagined in a million years that his first meeting with a galactic ruler would be a one-sided speech from the other side of a screen.

Guerra couldn't work with that.

He wasn't equipped to deal with this. He didn't *know* how to deal with this. Give him a tit-for-tat meeting, and he could bend the will of even the most staunch adversary.

But this—this was *insane*.

"I will keep this address brief," Dysart said. "I do not believe I owe you more than that."

He cleared his throat and said, "You are here for reasons that should be no surprise to you."

"Treason," Sterling said under his breath.

Guerra nodded, using air quotes to frame the context.

"And if you are surprised, then—well, I apologize for the mistake. But you know what they say about omelets, don't you? Consider yourself one of the unfortunate eggs."

A sharp, bloodless laugh emerged from the figure, but there was no humanity in it.

None at all.

"For the rest of you—for those who are clearly aware of your place in this situation—well, I guess congratulations are in order. You got your *wish*."

"Who the fuck would wish for this?" Coulson asked.

Guerra shushed him.

"You are a member of the so-called *resistance*. You are the cockroaches that destroy and shit on everything good and wholesome we have built here."

The leader stopped, composed himself.

"Which brings me to the main point. I don't want to leave you squirming in your seats for too long. I know how dreadfully *boring* these presentations can be. I used to be forced to sit through them myself."

He stepped back and sat down in a nearby chair. The camera followed him and zoomed in as he took his place. The new shot only showed him from the shoulders up, and he looked much more frail this way.

"You have infiltrated my organizations—cockroaches that you are—and sought to deconstruct them from the inside out. You fought to learn all the ARK's secrets, to quote-unquote liberate your fellow people."

He squinted, and his countenance became instantly menacing.

"Consider yourselves *free*. And the wages of liberation are death. I hope that's a fair trade-off. Even if it's not, that's exactly what's happening. This. Is. Real."

He seemed to take a curious amount of satisfaction in the statement, in acknowledging that he was murdering these people for defying his absolute rule.

But the glowering, gloating look did not slow him down. He continued after a brief, patient sigh.

"Oh, I imagine yourselves to be martyrs for your cause. But I can assure you: no one will know. No one will remember your names. No one will scream your names in the heat of a full-blown riot. No one will know about this place. It is an old theater, and one I've long imagined closing down. But I thought it would be nice to put on one last show, so—you're welcome."

The camera shifted slightly, zooming in to fill the entire screen with Dysart's taut, wicked face.

His smile widened, and he said, "Now that we have the prefatory pleasantries out of the way, let me tell you what's *really* going on. I mean, now that I know my secret will be safe with you always."

"I thought he said this was going to be brief," Coulson said.

"Shut—Up," Guerra replied.

"Beatrix—is a lie," he said. "There is no such person. Never was. She is a concoction made up by your organization to spread lies and undermine my administration."

Then, he seemed to consider something.

"Even if there was a young girl at the heart of all this, she is long gone, and not worth fighting for. And your rumors about the tests—that we are performing clinical trials of the mods you love so much on the dregs of society. Those who either could not or chose not to contribute to Xenograd in any meaningful way."

He coughed.

Herr Dysart didn't look good.

It was then that Guerra realized what set him apart from everyone they had seen so far.

He was *vibrating*, like a tuning fork set to a dog-high frequency.

Not shaking. He wasn't an addict in search of his next fix.

No, he was humming, his body producing a sound through disturbing the surrounding air molecules.

He's not well, Guerra thought.

It gave him a momentary glimpse, not into *what* the dictator was doing, but perhaps *why* he was doing it.

"By that," he continued, "I mean to say, useless eaters. Life unworthy of life, to quote an organization I personally admire. The shit under our feet, to put it another way."

At that, Dysart smiled sardonically.

Then, the iron-fisted ruler of Xenograd and captain of the ARK adjusted his lapels to show off his fake, nonexistent military achievements.

Once he was done with that, he leaned forward, so that only his eyes, nose, and mouth were visible in the frame. He looked like a floating set of human features.

"Bring out the sacks," he said, by way of conclusion. "Let's get started, boys. See you all in Hell."

End of transmission.

"Well," Coulson said, after a pause, "that was—something."

"It was proof," Sahana said, "of everything that's been floating around the United Galaxy for months."

"Did you get it?" Guerra asked.

"Every single moment," Sterling said. "When the comms station is up and running, I'll upload all of the video to the central server. No problem."

Sahana said, "If you want my opinion—"

"Always," Guerra responded.

"It would be far better for the rest of humanity if we just locked the doors behind us and never looked back."

"Well, we have to get to get to the comms station. Call for help."

At this, the mystic bristled. "Do we?"

"We can go back, wait for the UG to send help. It's far worse than we could have imagined. No one would fault you for that, Guerra. And they can't be *so* tied up with other administrative matters that they cannot come check on us."

He thought about it, thought about his lack of leadership thus far. This was what he had always been afraid of.

Not being able to rise to the occasion when the occasion demands it.

Then he looked across the faces of those under his charge, looked at the specific way they were measuring him up, seeing if he could do this.

And he stood firm.

"We stay," he said. "We stay, and we go to the comms station. If that's broken, then we reassess. Otherwise, we keep moving."

A loud *thump* echoed through the theater.

"Let's get going," Guerra said. "I don't think I want to know what's on the other side of that door."

"Too late," Katarina said quietly. "It's already here."

She raised her weapon, aiming for the theater's rear exit.

And then the door splintered into a thousand pieces.

24

The thing that appeared amidst the shards of the busted door—like many of the things Guerra had seen—could scarcely be described as human.

It was big, slimy, and...*undulating*. That was the only word that came to mind.

The creature perambulated via some kind of thudding shimmy, the musculature carrying it forward with heavy steps. It had two gigantic arms, with long-fingered hands dangling from the ends, and those hands seemed to reach for anything they came across.

From the way the skin sagged from the skull, the creature could have been wearing a human mask. Muscle slid from the bone. The eyes rolled around in the sockets like marbles, and the lips reared back to reveal blackened, rotting teeth.

As it approached, this giant inhuman thing, plodding though it was, yowled and screamed like it had been rectally penetrated with a saw blade.

"That's not Ebola," Guerra whispered, as the thing approached.

"Yeah, no shit," Coulson replied.

Katarina raised her rifle and dealt what would be a killing blow on any human begin in the universe, a shot square between the eyes.

But it did nothing.

Or seemed to do nothing, except piss the bastard off. Its head knocked backward, but the brain shot scarcely slowed it down. The thing just kept coming.

Guerra got a good look at Katarina's face in that moment. Her ever dead-pan expression had faltered. Like something had been taken away from her.

A moment of doubt, maybe.

Maybe in her abilities. Maybe in her own mortality. But Guerra saw weakness in her for perhaps the first time.

"Kat," he said. "Hit it again."

She looked up, saw him, and hesitated. Then, she nodded and raised the gun again.

This time, the bullet knocked the creature to its knees. A thick, ropey material oozed from the wound between its eyes, black and disgusting, but the thing didn't topple over.

Instead, it got up, staggered, and then continued stumbling forward. One of the claw-like hands snatched up a dead body from the theater chair and flung it at them.

They all ducked, and the body exploded in a spray of horrific, viscous material. It was like a biological dirty bomb, and it did the trick of confusing them.

They were still on the stage, so technically they held the high ground, but their defensive position left them vulnerable to a direct attack—which the thing was willing to give them.

Guerra scrambled to think of a response.

"Team," he said. "Unsling your weapons. Fire at will."

They did as he commanded, unleashing a fusillade of firepower on the creature below them.

The sludgy figure had just reached for another of the bodies, one hand clamping down on the burlap sack, when the bullets and force energy struck him like a fist.

The thing landed hard on its ass, temporarily stunned by the sheer wallop of the violence, and the body it had been holding slumped into the aisle.

The sack on the corpse's head opened up, and a long, gray whip-like shape slithered from the gap.

"Wait," Guerra said. "The snakes. The fucking snakes."

He didn't know if there was anything to it, but Sahana seemed to suggest a bite from one of these things would be deadly to a good-sized man.

Maybe it would work on a good-sized monster, too. He had to hope so, at the very least.

He pointed at the snake and said, "Kat, scare it back to him."

She nodded and fired a burst into the ground at the creature's feet.

The snake that had, until that moment, been slithering toward the stage, reared up and changed direction just as the sludgy creature attempted to find its feet.

Either the thing was just close enough—or the snake was just pissed off enough—but with a lightning quick movement, the black mamba snapped forward and struck at the creature.

The figure shrieked in surprise more than pain and then took out its frustration on the reptile. When he was done, the thing was in two pieces, and the creature was on its way toward them once again.

Katarina raised her weapon, intending on taking another shot, but Guerra waved it off.

He felt something that told him they should wait, and so he instructed her to do just that.

Katarina relaxed her finger on the trigger, but she didn't lower her weapon.

Moments later, the gray, gelatinous monster stopped, teetered, and then kind of collapsed sideways, hands clutching at its throat.

"My, that was fast," Sterling said.

Sahana replied: "The venom must work on those things more quickly. Something to do with their circulation and metabolism, maybe?"

"You fucking got me," Coulson added. "I'm just glad it worked."

Coulson was the first off the stage. Guerra meant to tell him to give it a few minutes, but his voice was caught in his throat.

Still, he was proud of himself for holding off, when he very well could have wasted ammunition. Ammunition he thought they would certainly need before this whole mission was done.

"Be careful, Coulson," Sahana said, and the foul-mouthed medic raised a hand in acknowledgment.

As he stood over the corpse of the sludgy figure, he said, "Man, this thing is fucking u-g-l-y. Like, I wonder if it was *ever* really human."

I hope we don't stay long enough to figure out, Guerra found himself thinking. He didn't know if he believed it, but his thoughts were way ahead of his rational mind right now.

And as Coulson stood there, hands on hips, Guerra wondered what was going to happen next.

Coulson knelt and pulled his pack from his shoulders. He pulled the torch from its holster and dug around beneath that.

"Going to get a sample," he said, as if anyone had asked him. "I've got this testing equipment that can tell us—"

And then it happened.

The creature twitched.

Coulson snapped his attention back to where it should have been, but he was a split second too late.

The thing reached one massive hand for Coulson's throat and stood up at the same time. It raised Coulson aloft like some curious toy—and just *squeezed*.

The only sound Guerra could hear over the rapid beating of his heart was the clicking sound in the back of Coulson's throat. Something essential sounded like it was being crushed.

Kate raised her weapon.

"Hold your fire," Guerra said. "You might hit Coulson. Let him handle it."

"But he's turning purple," Sterling said.

The adrenaline surge of commanding his crew was superseded by his need to enforce it.

"It's an order," Guerra said. "Follow it."

Meanwhile, Coulson was in the fight of his life. Kicking his feet.

Feebly swinging his arms. All the while, the life was being squeezed right out of him.

The creature reached its other slimy hand up, grabbing for the top of Coulson's head—presumably to separate it from his body—when something happened.

Coulson's torched clicked on.

It was powerful enough to split a diamond in two, and he'd somehow managed to hang onto it in the lead-up to this fight's climax.

The flame from the torch burned white-hot, and it distracted the creature long enough to keep it from decapitating their crew mate.

And Coulson wasted no time.

The moment he could, he raised the torch and jammed it into one of the sludgy creature's lolling marble eyes.

It screamed—this one an order of magnitude louder and more pained than the previous ones—and Coulson reacted by screaming, too.

But his scream was not out of pain.

It was pure fury.

The man's eyes danced with a combination of anger and joy, and he continued to carve out the thing's face even after he'd been dropped to the ground.

Something in the creature's nervous system must have shut down, because it just kind of stood there and twitched as Coulson burned a hole in its skull.

Guerra knew it was all over when he saw the fire from the torch open up a gaping wound in the back of the thing's head.

The creature's knees buckled just as Coulson let out a whoop of victory, and so he didn't see the thing topple over on him.

They both collapsed to the ground, Coulson underneath, as the slimy figure retched out its death rattle onto Coulson's helmet. It burped up a gooey black substance as its body finally gave way, and then everything in the theater was still.

"A little help!" he screamed. "This stuff tastes like dirty toilet water. Please, God! Fucking *help!*"

25

When they emerged from the theater's bowels, Sterling stopped them to check the map again.

"We're close," he said. "And, we're avoiding a lot of the main thoroughfares, so it's less dangerous."

Coulson barked laughter and pointed at a dead body.

"Whoop-de-doo," he said, nudging the figure's meaty tricep with one boot toe.

And then, his face changed.

"Hold on," he said.

Coulson knelt next to the body and pulled a small medical case from his pack.

"What are you doing?" Guerra asked.

"I just had an idea, rare as that may seem. Give me a second."

Coulson pulled a syringe from the case and lifted the body's backside. Beneath the figure was a long-coagulated pool of blood. It had settled where the body fell and gathered there in the back, slowly seeping out as the flesh deteriorated.

Coulson carefully inserted it into the member of the dead and used one thumb to drain some dark red fluid from the body. The smell that wafted from it was mind-alteringly bad.

"I could use a swab," he said, "but the blood—even old blood—gives much more precise results."

A sound like angry dinosaurs erupted from somewhere down the street, and Katarina said, "Better hurry. I think I hear some of our friends coming this way."

"Hold on," Coulson said. "This will only take a second, I swear."

Next, he pulled a small, rectangular device from the kit and inserted the syringe into its side. The item beeped three times and then went silent again.

"Now what?" Sterling asked.

"Now—we wait," he said. "I need to keep this thing still while it performs the necessary tests. That's all."

"What does it *do*?"

This was Sterling again.

"Checks any substance for genetic material and then analyzes it. I can find out if the decedent snorted painkillers three decades ago. This thing is *balanced*."

"Oh," Sterling said, another question balanced on the edge of his lips.

Meanwhile, Guerra stepped away from the group.

"Where are you headed?" Sahana asked.

Guerra smiled and turned back to her. "The store," he said.

"It's not safe," she said, adding, "to be alone out there."

"I'll be fine," he replied. "You need anything?"

She gave him a curious look and shook her head, but she didn't say anything else.

Perhaps she understood.

That was the problem. It seemed like she understood *too much*. She always seemed to have a grasp on any given situation, and he didn't want that.

Not right now.

He needed a moment alone.

A moment to get his thoughts together, at the very least.

He had spent the last few hours living from moment-to-moment–*surviving* moment-to-moment—so he needed to gain some perspective.

This was *his* gig, after all.

Or was supposed to be.

He didn't feel quite like the man of the hour. Everything had crumbled around him—around *all* of them—and so it would be a miracle if they just walked out of here alive.

But he couldn't fail.

If he failed *here*—even with the clusterfuck they had encountered—there was no way he would move up the ranks in the United Galaxy.

This was the path for people like him. It was really the *only* path, if he wanted to reach a position of power.

And he did. He wanted to ride the escalator all the way to the top. He had aspirations to earn a job as an Under Secretary of...something.

Anything, really. It wasn't the job itself that mattered. The title. None of that was what drove him.

Perhaps that was the problem. He just wanted to be *something*. He imagined it was difficult to grow up as nothing on Earth.

Oh, but how that feeling was magnified in space. When set perpetually against the backdrop of the infinite majesty of space, one couldn't help but feel utterly worthless in the grand scheme of things.

Where he had grown up, there was no stock placed in achievement. Or advancement. On his ship, there was just the toil of everyday life, pointless and meandering, waiting out the hours until the last grains of sand in the hourglass gave way, leaving the husk of one's body behind.

There was just the adherence to religion—to the things The Good Book espoused—and that was that.

When he first mentioned that he might be going away to train for the UG Fleet, his father had scoffed.

"Rearranging deck chairs on the *Titanic*," his father had said.

An old reference for an old man.

His father hadn't believed in him.

No.

It was much more fundamental than that. The old man hadn't believed in *anything*—save for the spiritual.

He was hard-hearted and heavy-handed. Guerra had sometimes worn the results of discipline's watermark on his face when he ventured into public.

He had not wanted to spare the old man the embarrassment. Still, he had dreamed.

Of getting away.

Of turning his back on everything he had suffered.

On God Himself.

Or his father.

Same thing.

Either way, he'd known at a very young age he couldn't remain. He had to get out. Had to detach his horse from that particular cart and hitch up to one that was built for something else.

So he guessed he had joined the UG as much to rebel against the anti-establishment posturing of his family as much as anything.

But then *it* had happened.

The thing—oh, the thing.

The thing he'd had to hide from everyone—including upper management at the UG.

Still, the silhouette of his father remained with him, the plainspoken, rugged man who looked at least a decade older than his years even when he was a young man.

The angry, weathered face, sneering at ambition. Contemptuous of all worldly things.

Guerra became so enamored with the mental image of his father, he almost smacked face-first into the glass door of the nearest shop.

With an effortless but nevertheless heavy gesture, he shouldered through a chain-locked door and went around the store's main counter.

There, he found exactly what he had come looking for.

Behind the counter, there was the typical assortment of beverages, but there was also one of those...vending machines.

A *Mod Machine*.

And this one appeared to be intact.

He touched the machine's main screen, which produced a cute, well-rendered animation. The figure in front of him was a scantily-clad woman, artificially buxom.

"Hey, there, big fella," she said in a faux-noir voice. "You looking for a date, or a mod?"

He chose *mod*, and then watched the screen flip, as a whole host of options appeared before him. There was an icon for each option, and each was highly colorful.

Guerra read the names and descriptions for the mods. Many of them were grayed out, indicating they were sold out, but others remained highlighted.

Brain Bullet
Why use your muscles to move things, when you can use your *mind*?

Heart Helper
Need some assistance finding your mate attractive? This can give you a change of *heart*.

Muscle Mask
Get a temporary boost to make it through your work shift with this mighty mod.

Guerra had never seen anything like this before, but it seemed to fit the overall philosophy of Xenograd's underlying premise.

Better living through chemistry.

If Dysart believed his people to be superior to the other human beings in he galaxy, then perhaps this experiment was him writing a check for his ass to cash.

Guerra looked around.

Seems like he might have overdrafted, Guerra thought.

Still, he was interested in the whole idea. Take a mass-produced elixir and eradicate some unwanted aspect of yourself—it was intoxicating.

It brought up so many questions, but if they stayed long enough, maybe they would get answered.

As he searched through this vending machine of genetic potions, Guerra felt the presence of someone—or something—behind him.

It was a momentary flash, but it sent chills racing up his spine.

His mind had time to produce a single sliver of hope as he turned, one hand reaching for his force gun.

Then, the smell hit him, and he realized—a second too late—that it was not Coulson playing a sick prank on him. Nor was it Katarina sneaking over to protect him.

Something had crawled out of the gutter—or the grave—and found him all by his lonesome.

The force gun was in his hand when he saw the thing, but it didn't stay there for long. The creature slapped it out of his possession and the went for Guerra's throat.

It was then he got a good look at it. The skin had sloughed off like day-old fried chicken, and the meat beneath was rotten and irritated.

As they toppled over, Guerra struggled to keep the hands from clawing out his eyes.

But that left the mouth wide open. The thing's teeth came snapping at him, and he could only hope that he wouldn't die this way, with some undead creature ripping out his jugular on the floor of this dirty, abandoned old store.

He shrieked, as much out of desperation as terror, and used the last of his strength to push the thing up, hoping he might be able to roll sideways out from under it.

Just then—just as the head was thrust into a blade of light—the whole top of the skull was ripped away as if pulled by a heavy cable, and the figure fell limply sideways.

Guerra glanced up to see Coulson standing there, rifle in hand, a ghostly, shellshocked look on his face.

"Thought I—well, shit, I was just coming to see what you'd gotten into. Looks like a lot."

"I—thank you, Coulson," Guerra said, getting slowly to his feet. The blood was still warm on his uniform. "I—I don't know how to repay you."

He wasn't shocked that Coulson would save his life. It was part of the code, and even though the foul-mouthed medic was rude, he wasn't without scruples.

"You can repay me by not getting yourself fucking *killed*," he said in his usual brash tone, but there was something missing in it.

He was scared.

Coulson was wearing an angry mask, but that's all it was—a mask.

And it terrified him. He could put on his best Billy Badass impression, but Guerra saw through that. He just hoped that Coulson knew, because then he might tone it down a little bit.

"How's the test going?"

"Still going," Coulson replied.

"Well, then. Come with me."

They stepped over the dead body and made their way to the Mod Machine. It was a big red box, kind of the soda vendors they used to have back on Earth, and even though it had been knocked sideways—vandals—Guerra was almost certain it was fully functional.

Guerra restarted the process of choosing a mod, and Coulson looked over his shoulder at the giant screen.

"I wonder how these are administered," Guerra pondered aloud. "An injection? A pill?"

"Suppository?" Coulson offered. "Makes it easy, if you yourself are an asshole."

Guerra ignored the jab. "These aren't for personal use," he said. "These are for the workers. It's all about *building* here on the ARK"

"Except for *Heart Helper*," Coulson replied. "Sounds like the ARK government was going all-in on creating super subjects."

"Agreed."

"I mean, if you read between the lines, it certainly looks like they were forcing people to have kids for the sake of the government and the populace. It's some real *1984* stuff, if you ask me."

Going down the line, he looked at the rest of the mods. They *did* have a sort of...totalitarian flair about them, and Guerra felt a knot loosen in his guts. He wondered how much money—how much time—was spent convincing these people they *needed* these little perks.

"And yet," Coulson said, from over Guerra's shoulder, "not one of these perks says it will turn you into an undead monster. Guess it's a crap shoot, eh?"

"That's not a mod thing," Guerra said, though he wasn't sure.

"Guess we're going to find out," Coulson replied, and then he walked away. "I'm headed back."

Guerra continued to stare at the screen. He felt something—a connection almost made—between the mods themselves and the beasts running amok on the ship.

Eventually, though, the glare of the screen made his eyes hurt. And besides, he didn't have time to play around with these authoritarian toys.

"Huh," Guerra said, at last, and then he returned to where they awaited the genetic tests.

When he got back, the rest of the crew was hovering over the testing kit, their eyes as wide as decency would allow.

"Who died?" Guerra asked, and they all turned their heads to face him.

Coulson's mouth gaped open, and he said, "Whatever's infected the people on this ship—it..."

"What?"

"It ain't human."

26

Guerra had to make sure he caught his breath before he articulated the thought that formed in his brain.

"What do you mean '*ain't human?*'"

"I mean, like, this machine went absolutely crazy when the results came up. And like I said: it's not human."

"How do you know?"

"All human lifeforms are carbon-based, right?"

"Right."

Guerra felt his stomach shrink.

"Well, the blood and DNA from these specimens are composed mostly of silicon."

"Could it be a problem with—"

"My ability to extract DNA? Nossir."

He said it like one word: *nossir*.

"These...people are filled with silicon dioxide. Silica, as it is more commonly known."

Guerra regarded the body at their feet and sighed.

"What conclusion can we draw from it?"

"Well," Coulson said, returning the testing kit to his pack and standing up, "if I were a betting man, I'd say our authoritarian host was up to his elbows in alien material."

"Yeah," Guerra echoed.

"And however he found it, he's using it on his people to an alarming degree. They have to have been driven crazy by it."

Guerra thought about that, too. "Do you think it could have anything to do with the mods?"

"I'd say almost *definitely*," Coulson replied.

Sterling and the others nodded too.

"Which means we can't go shooting that shit up like steroids," Coulson said, "unless you want to become like one of them. And—personally—I don't."

Sahana stepped into the circle of illumination provided by the nearby neon lights and said, "That must be what Dysart meant when he discussed the tests."

Guerra nodded. "Must be."

Sterling and Katarina nodded, as well.

"Whatever Dysart did," Sahana continued, "it shifted the balance too far to one side, and now all the pent-up evil from this place has spilled into the void."

Sterling seemed confused. "Which means—"

"Which means that Pandora's fucking box is open," Coulson finished, "and all the worst possible outcomes of his playing God are happening right now."

Sterling looked to Sahana, who nodded. "It's the energy I must have felt coming in."

"And the name that sat upon him was Death," Guerra whispered.

The rest of the group looked at him.

Guerra cleared his throat. "It's, uh—it's a verse from the Bible," he said.

"Oh, that old chestnut," Coulson said. "Thank Jeebus for what he's done here."

"Shut up, Coulson," Sahana said. "I want to hear it. The rest of it. There's more, right?"

Guerra nodded. "And power was given unto them over the fourth part of the earth, to kill with sword, and with hunger, and with death, and with the beasts of the earth."

"Revelation?" Sahana asked.

"Yes."

"Come on," Coulson said. "Do you really think this is some dead-guy-on-a-cross thing?"

Guerra shook his head. "I was—I was just remembering something. In the time before we lived up here."

"You don't *remember* the time before," Coulson argued.

No, but he had visions. He had dreams. There was something fundamentally wrong with the way humanity no longer lived among the trees and the oceans and the animals native to human experience.

"Maybe you're right," Guerra said. "Maybe there is no God. Maybe this is all just humanity playing itself out."

"Or maybe God just forgot about us," Sahana said. "All of us. Every single human being."

"Unless this was the plan all along," Sterling replied.

"What do you mean?" Guerra asked.

"Think about it. All the people down here—they represent the others, the proletariat, the untouchables. Maybe Dysart and his rich, powerful buddies got what they wanted out of these...experiments, and now they've walled themselves off from the rest of the ship. Maybe they've *forgotten* about what's happening down here because they don't *have* to remember."

"Speaking of Dysart," Coulson said, "where is that fucker?"

Guerra looked over at Coulson.

"What do you mean?"

"He knows we're here," Coulson replied. "You say he's forgotten about his people, his society. But you can't tell me he's conveniently forgotten about *us*."

Guerra said, "He probably thinks his *minions* will take care of us. I mean, it's not likely that we will make it out of this alive."

"Don't say that," Sterling said. "Don't say it."

"It's true," Sahana said. "We cannot succeed in this until we know what failure looks like."

"I think being murdered by half-alien psychopaths is a pretty clear picture of failure," Coulson said. "No offense."

Off in the distance, one of *them* shrieked. It was terrifying sound, yes, but there was also something else in it. To Guerra, the sound was almost a cry of—loneliness.

Katarina snapped her fingers, and Guerra turned to see her motion them away from their spot. Surely, if they stayed in placed, they would almost certainly die.

"Where to next, partner?" Coulson asked Sterling.

"The Xenograd History Museum," Sterling replied. "Otherwise known as the indoctrination camp for this ship."

"Beautiful," Coulson replied. "Can't wait."

"And not for nothing," Sterling said, "but it's a hell of a lot worse than you think it might be."

"Like I said," Coulson replied, "'can't wait."

27

After they had traveled a ways, the new kid seemed to tire of his computer program, because he just started talking.

"We should name them," Sterling said. "These things should have names, right? We can't call them *the monsters*, and we sure as hell can't call them *people*."

"Why not?" Guerra asked. "That's what they are."

"What?" Coulson said. "Monsters?"

"No," Guerra replied. "People."

"That's what they *were*," Coulson said. "Now, they're just zombie...aliens."

Guerra rolled his eyes. He said, "You're not suggesting that we—"

"No," Coulson said. "I would never—"

"But you just did."

"Listen," Coulson said. "It just came out that way. I mean, I'm right, though. We have to call these things *something*. It's like—what are we going to call them in the reports?"

No one spoke for a moment.

"Let's face it," Coulson continued. "There *will* be reports. Paperwork galore. Lots and lots of it."

"He's right," Sterling replied. "I mean, even in shorthand, it would be nice to have a name for them. I don't think want to be attacked by one and have to *think* about what's attacking me."

"Yeah," Coulson said, "you'll be too busy screaming and shitting your suit."

Sterling shrugged. "Probably," he said.

"No judgment," Coulson replied. "I'll probably do the same if one of them gets its teeth into me."

Sterling, perhaps buoyed by the fact that Coulson hadn't immediately attacked him, laughed and said, "How about—Modsters?"

Coulson laughed out loud. "That's the silliest shit I've ever heard in my life, kid."

"Just a suggestion," Sterling replied. "What's *your* idea, Coulson?"

"Well," Coulson said, clearly having no idea, "I was thinking that, since we're on the ARK, we call them ARKians."

It was Sterling's turn to laugh.

"Shut the fuck up, kid," Coulson said. "Nobody asked you. I think it's a good name."

Guerra waited for the laughter to subside, and then he said, "Kharisiri."

"The fuck is that?" Coulson asked.

"In my homeland," Guerra said, "or at least my descendants' homeland, there is a beast they call the Kharisiri. Some people call it a Pishtaco, but my grandmother, she always called it the Kharisiri."

"What is it?" Sterling asked.

"It's a beast that roams the mountains and feeds on local villagers."

"Sounds about right."

"It's usually portrayed as an outsider. It was originally a metaphor for white people. You know—the invading hordes."

They all let that sink in.

Then, Sahana said, "The people they're doing testing on—they're the outsiders. They're not invaders."

But Sterling raised a finger. He was on to something. He said, "So it's an inversion of the original meaning, but it still fits. How did you say it?"

"Kharisiri."

"It's kind of long," Coulson said.

"It doesn't have to be *the* name," Guerra said. "It was more—I guess it just made me think of my homeland."

"I get it," Sterling replied.

"Maybe not that," Guerra said. "We don't have to call them Kharisiri, though that's what I'll think whenever we encounter them."

Coulson looked annoyed. "Then what *do* we call them?"

They sat there for an extended time.

Then, Guerra said, "Well, maybe not Modsters—"

"Makes them sound like a mode of transportation," Sahana said.

Guerra nodded.

"But maybe we can call them—modders?" he said.

They all looked at one another.

Sterling smiled. "I like it. As much as I can like anything in this horrible, misbegotten fucking place."

"I accept it," Sahana said.

Guerra glanced at Katarina, whose eyes were fixed on a point on the distant horizon. She nodded.

"Okay, then," Coulson said. "Modders, it is."

They walked in silence for a time, and then they came to an impossibly elaborate building, a gaudy monstrosity that stretched as wide and as tall as their eyes could see.

"Here is the indoctrination center," Sterling said. "Just where the map said it would be. There's only one problem."

"And what's that?"

Sterling clicked on his helmet lamp and pointed it to the left.

"The entrance is right there."

"I don't see—oh. Oh, God."

Where there should have been an entrance, there was instead a giant wall of—

"Are those—are those *bodies*?"

Sterling nodded. "They must have been trying to get into the museum, for some reason."

"And—what—they killed one another in a human stampede?" Coulson asked.

Sterling shrugged. "That's more your area of expertise than mine. I just know that the door to get in is right where all those bodies have been piled."

Guerra said, "That's got to be at least a hundred people, all piled up like corded wood."

Coulson shook his head. "It looks like one of those videos of people trying to escape a building that's on fire."

Guerra walked over to the mound of flesh. "Coulson, can you get a bead on what happened?"

Coulson looked from the dead bodies to Guerra. "You really want me to do this, *hombre*?"

Guerra ignored the slight. "Yes, I do."

"Because I don't think getting a cause of death will do anything to help us—"

"Just do it," Guerra said, and stepped away.

The medic murmured something under his breath, but Guerra decided to ignore that, too.

The machine beeped a few minutes later, and Coulson knelt down to sort out its results.

Once he realized what the data meant, he said, "Oh, boy. That's—that's not good."

"What is it?" Sahana asked. "What are they doing here?"

"Well," Coulson replied, "I don't know the answer to that question. But I do know what killed them."

"And what's that?" Guerra asked.

He met Guerra's gaze and said, "They've been gassed."

"How do you know that?"

"Heightened levels of trace compounds, like ricin and—"

Coulson screamed and jumped back. He crab-walked back toward them as everyone else drew a weapon. Katarina stepped in front of them all, aiming for the center mass of the body collective.

"What is it?" Sahana asked.

"One of them moved," Coulson said, his voice shaking. "One of them fucking *moved*, and I'm not hallucinating."

But no one dared to check. No one, save for Katarina, that was. She glided forward, like a bug on water, and stopped just a few feet shy of the pile.

She clicked her headlamp, and for the longest time, she scanned the area, using the gun as a guide.

Guerra himself stared at them without blinking until his eyes blurred, but he didn't see anything, either.

"I'm fucking telling you," Coulson protested, "I saw something move. It was an arm or a leg or a head or something. But one of those bodies *moved*."

"Whatever it was," Katarina said, "it's not moving now."

"Yeah, no shit."

Guerra was possessed of a specific impulse, one that he could not quite put down the way he had his other verbal impulses.

"Coulson, are you sure that's what you saw?"

Coulson glared at him. "Of course I'm fucking sure that's what I saw. What the fuck else would it be?"

He didn't seem to catch Guerra's drift, and maybe Guerra wasn't being unequivocal, so he cleared his throat and said exactly what was on his mind.

"Listen, there's a chance it could be something else. You know? This place is shadowy, and besides, I know you've had issues with substance abuse in the past, and—"

"This isn't fucking junkie behavior, Guerra," Coulson said, looking from him to the rest of them. "Jesus *Christ*, man. I hope you'd have more discretion than *this*."

Guerra felt his face grow how with shame and embarrassment, but he did not back down.

"I'm sorry," he found himself saying, despite the words rolling over and over in his brain. "I spoke out of turn."

"You're goddamned right you did," he replied.

But his mind already seemed to be working on something else. He was reaching delicately through the pile of limbs, and then when he found was he was looking for, he bounded backward and turned away from them.

"What is it? What did you find."

"All the people on top, they're adults, but the kids—the kids are all underneath. The adults—I assume some of them were parents—they trampled all the kids, trying to get inside."

His voice was high-pitched and rough, as though he had somehow strained it. In fact, it didn't sound much like Coulson whatsoever to Guerra.

Sahana asked, "What does that tell you?"

Guerra thought about it. "Whatever was out here with them—whatever did this to them—was one hell of a terrifying thing."

"Maybe the big monster?" Sterling asked.

It was possible. Guerra was almost positive that if *he* saw the thing slithering around in the shadows of this place, he might trample someone to get away, too.

"Yeah," Guerra said, "we definitely need to get the hell—"

The sentence was interrupted by a horrific volley of gunfire from Katarina, who sent rounds from her machine gun into the flesh pressed against the entrance. The rounds echoed in the wide open space with horrifying clarity.

The others joined in, firing their force weapons at the collection of bodies. Katarina didn't stop until the whole of her clip was gone, and when she finished, she calmly popped it free and replaced it with a fresh one.

Guerra, in that moment, though, had seen something in Katarina's eyes that unsettled him.

It was fear.

Fear, yes—or maybe *confusion*.

Katarina was not the sort to do anything unprovoked. It was one of the reasons Guerra trusted her. She fired her weapon only for cause. In other words, it was never an accident for her to pull the trigger.

And yet she had.

Once they seemed to have filled their bloodlust, each of them, in turn, released the trigger on their weapons.

The sound of silence in the wake of all that firing was deafening.

"Jesus *Christ*," Coulson said. "What was that all about?"

"Thought I saw something," she said, as if that were a sufficient enough explanation. "Guess I was wrong."

And then she walked away, leaving them all to pick up the pieces of what had just happened.

Coulson was the first to break the confused silence.

"Let's see if we can find another way in," he said. "I don't want to be out here any longer than I have to. New kid, do you have any bead on that?"

He checked his maps and nodded.

They all abandoned the mound of flesh like it were a tourist attraction that no longer interested them.

Then, a long, low moan, like rusted metal settling in an old building seemed to make the whole ship shudder.

28

Once the bone-jarring noise came to a slow and ominous silence, each of them, to a person, turned to face the other.

He couldn't tell what *they* were thinking, but he knew exactly what *he* was thinking.

His mind conjured up all sorts of images, none of them good. Again, he thought of *The Leviathan*, recalling the days of his childhood, when his parents forced him to read The Bible *ad nauseam*, and he would find himself crossing paths with some perpetually nightmarish story from the Old Testament.

Whether it was God's ceaseless torment of Job or Elisha calling up two bears kill children for mocking his baldness, Guerra found a never-ending fountain of blood and gore emanating from the one book from which his parents derived existential solace.

And then there was The Leviathan.

The ancient beast that roamed the depths of the sea. It wasn't involved in God's massacres of the innocents. Nor was it the subject of some protracted revelation about the world's end.

And yet it terrified Guerra more than any other story.

It was in the idea of the Leviathan that Guerra found God Himself, a boundless being capable of swallowing civilizations whole, capable of untold amounts of violence.

And this was what his parents *believed* in?

Meanwhile, back on the ARK, the crew had turned and was staring in the beast's direction.

"And there's *that* thing," Coulson said. "What the fuck *is* it?"

"Sounds like a space whale," Sterling said. "Or, like, a space squid. Do giant squids make noise?"

"We will not be here long enough to find out," Sahana said.

"I hope not," Guerra said.

"We really need to get out of here," Sahana replied. "I feel the darkness getting ever closer."

"And so are we," Guerra said. "Closer to our exit. I promise. The comms station is just on the other side of this museum. Right, Sterling?"

"Right."

"Okay, then," Guerra said. "We repair it, and we're out. Done deal."

Sahana gave him a wry, pained look, but she said nothing.

Katarina just pointed her gun in the direction of the sound. Her eyes indicated she would just *love* to die fighting something so big, a challenge worthy of her talents.

"Come on," Guerra said. "Sterling, lead on."

They walked in silence for some time. Guerra figured they were all thinking about the giant monster hiding in the shadows—*he* certainly was—but he didn't want to break the spell of their silence. It gave him time to think.

Finally, Coulson said, "What the fuck are they going to do here? Like, what is going to happen to this place when word finally gets out?"

Guerra considered it.

"There will have to be trials," he said. "Testimony. This will drag on for *years*, if I know the UG as well as I think I do."

"And meanwhile these assholes will be on house arrest, watching their ship turn into a piece of flying rubble."

"The rich get richer, and the poor get laid off," Sahana said. "That's just the way the world's always worked."

"Doesn't make it right," Coulson muttered under his breath.

"Is that where your anger comes from? The idea that things are not fair? That it?"

"You goddamned right that's it," Coulson said. "That's why new kid over there has to earn his stripes."

"Oh, because you do such a good job of that with the others," Guerra said.

"Watch it, *pendejo*," Coulson said, mocking Guerra's heritage. "I still haven't forgiven you for the drug addict comment yet."

"Fair enough," Guerra replied, adding, "*pendejo.*"

The medic smiled grimly, despite his best efforts to do the opposite.

Sahana said, "Personally, I do not believe in revenge and retaliation. It is bad for the blood, bad for the soul."

"Fucking good for *you*," Coulson said. "I think these motherfuckers deserve the worst of what's coming to 'em."

"That is where you and I differ," Sahana said.

"Oh, it definitely is," Coulson replied. "Whatever we're calling these things—"

"Modders," Guerra said. "Or—if you like the symbolism—Kharisiri."

"Fine. Yeah. Whatever. Maybe we *should* just let them mop the whole ship up. Just lock the door behind us and let old Darwin have his way. Am I right?"

Sahana blushed, and Guerra held up a hand to silence Coulson, but he was on a roll. so he didn't even notice.

"Or maybe they should just send them back to Earth," Coulson said. "If you can't handle living life the way we've all agreed to do it, then you should make it on your own."

"The Earth is one big nuclear Christmas," Sterling said. "You'd last about ten seconds before your body turned into a giant tumor."

"How do we know that," Coulson replied. "Huh? Have you seen it with your own two eyes?"

"I don't have to experience something to know it's true. Why else would we be living up here, when there's a whole planet down there, where we are *meant* to live?"

"I don't know," Coulson replied, sounding very annoyed. "Maybe the UG's been lying to us the same way Dysart's been lying to *his* people."

Guerra blew out an irritated puff of air. "That's ridiculous," he said.

Then again, he didn't have any evidence to back it up, either. "You can see with your own eyes that our home planet is absolutely unlivable."

"So far as we *know*," Coulson said.

"Oh," Guerra replied. "I knew you were an asshole, but I didn't know you were a conspiracy theorist, too."

Common wisdom throughout the galaxy was that Earth had been rendered uninhabitable by—an event.

It was rarely spoken of, and even then in hushed tones out of absolute necessity. Like a murderer in the family.

It was possible to view the planet through a high-powered telescopic lens, but those were few and far between, and not available on every ship.

And so, of course, there had always been rumors about Earth.

It was actually a secret military base.

That it had been rendered uninhabitable through secret mind-control experiments.

Some even believed it was made of cheese.

But the conspiratorial wing of the human population took up no more—*no more*—than twenty-five percent, tops. It made elections somewhat tricky, but since there was very little need to invade physical spaces, there was no gerrymandering, and so popular vote elections had taken precedence.

There was the occasional, wrong-headed uprising, but those were quelled fairly quickly—usually by the UG.

Allowing such widespread theories served a few important functions. First of all, they provided an air vent for the crazies to get out their fears. And two, they gave the governments something to use as a means for identifying and filtering out those crazies.

The conspiracies had been worse on Earth.

The internet was a new technology back then, and because the un-evolved parts of the brain kept pumping dopamine into their forefathers' bodies, things got—weird.

Whole populations turned on one another. Brother fought brother—online, at least.

Objective truth became a thing of the past. Partisan bickering and one-upsmanship displaced the necessary functions of parliamentary procedure and legitimate governance.

And that was how things began to go downhill quickly. The internet—as it was then called—provided people with the privilege of living in self-installed echo chambers.

Soon, it was like people of different political or socioeconomic persuasions were speaking different languages.

And then The Event happened.

Guerra didn't know much about it. Nobody did. But no one could point to the exact cause which had hastened humanity's migration to space.

Everything calmed down for a long time.

"Guerra?"

He snapped out of it—his funk—and returned to the moment.

"Sorry," he said. "I got sidetracked by—"

"How fucking incompetent you are?"

Guerra looked at him sharply, but Coulson was smiling, so he let it go.

"Well," Guerra concluded, "we won't solve this discussion anytime soon. But once we're back on the ship—"

"You've got yourself a fucking bet," Coulson said. "I'll prove to you—somehow—that our bosses are lying to us about Earth."

Sterling cut them both off by saying, "Here we are. We can go through this way."

"What is this place?"

"This is the far less public—and less desirable—entrance to the museum. If I had to guess, I would say it was meant for the, uhm, *lesser* populations aboard the ARK."

"The modders," Guerra said.

"Right," Sterling replied, looking up at the giant sign above them. It read—

The Covenant
A BRIEF HISTORY OF XENOGRAD

"Clever," Coulson sneered.

The door was locked, but the butt of Coulson's weapon made quick work of it.

Once all were inside, Sterling found a series of switches and flipped them. The building came alive, and the illumination revealed yet another scene of despicable horror.

Above them, where the signs welcomed customers, a person had been stripped naked and nailed to the front half of a boat, aptly titled *The ARK*.

Not only had the clothes been taken from the body, the skin had been peeled off, as well. Everything, from the eyelids and the ears down to the fingernails and genitals, had been gruesomely extracted.

"What's the symbolism?" Coulson asked.

"It's a crucifixion," Guerra said.

"That's not my area of expertise," Sahana said.

"Mine, either," Guerra replied. "I just know that it's a desecration of what some people believe."

"The question is," Sahana said, "why would he do *this*? The people of Xenograd aren't Christians."

Guerra replied, "Maybe it's like the other torture we've seen. A warning from antiquity, but not necessarily pointing to any particular liturgy."

Sahana thought about it. Finally, she said, "All beings tremble before death. Why take it to this extreme?"

Coulson said, "Because he is a *nutbag*. We don't need to psychoanalyze the insane, do we? Unless we want to become *just like* the asshole. I mean—fuck—look at this."

Bodies had been positioned like grotesque art installations throughout the museum's ground floor. Like they had been placed there *just* for them.

Guerra wished he could avert his eyes, but he knew better. This was his burden to bear. If he wanted to be the arbiter of justice in this place, then he had to be able to endure the worst of its suffering.

Katarina stepped over to one of the tableaus of death—looking very much like a melted red candle—and plucked the placard hanging around the decedent's neck.

She handed it to Sahana, who said the single, etched word aloud: "ROACH."

"Dehumanizing them," Guerra said. "Gives him cause to do this. Or *justification*, I should say."

From the other side of the room, Sterling held up another placard. "This one says, 'THE UNWANTED.'"

Guerra fought to stay objective. "Do you see anything about them that might tell us their origins?"

Sterling said, "The UG tried to keep records on trading habits of the people of the ARK, but of course those could have been falsified. Still, I don't see *anything* about them acquiring people."

"So he didn't officially engage in slavery," Coulson said. "What a fucking revelation."

"That's not what I'm saying," Sterling replied. "I'm saying that *the records* don't indicate it, but *they* may not be be accurate."

"Interesting," Coulson said, wandering off.

Meanwhile, Sahana was busily typing something on a nearby terminal.

"I think I can get it up and running," she said, "and maybe we can figure out the nature of the propaganda they were selling to their own people."

"Wouldn't it be the same thing they tried to sell to the UG?" Sterling asked.

"Not necessarily," Sahana replied. "The public-facing diplomacy could very well—Ah, here we go!"

The ceiling-mounted projector whirred to life, and though it crackled and jumped for a minute before picking up in the middle of the propaganda video.

> It was during initial expansion—in which supplies were traded among the many ships in the post-Earth fleet—that The Founder was born. Hadrian Dysart—statesman, scholar, scientist, soldier, husband, and father—grew up in one of the poorest tenements in Xenograd and rose to political prominence when he discovered existence of the ship's castaways.
>
> You see, museum-goers, there was a time when the world of the Ark was pure and pristine. It was absolutely unsoiled by the grime of human contamination, and thanks to the efforts of our Dear Leader, Hadrian Dysart, it may be that way again.
>
> But I'm getting ahead of myself. Let me take a step back to explain the election of the one and only, Dysart.
>
> For a time on the Ark, there existed a horrific famine, in which a quarter of the ship's population starved to death due to lack of food. Part of it had to do with the bureaucracy in the corrupt and evil government presiding over the people at that time, and the other half was the result of an unsettling discovery, led by then-unknown Hadrian Dysart.
>
> Dysart made his political hay by bringing to light the existence of The Stowaways, a term he used to describe non-Ark personnel, but one that is no longer used on the ship.
>
> Dysart gained prominence in the political movement at the time by pointing out the irony of feeding people with impure blood, when that food could go to much more deserving—and much more pure —descendants of the Earth system.
>
> Here is an excerpt from an early video shot during the presidential election, just before Dysart's first term in office.

When Dysart appeared as a hologram, he was filmed from a low angle, giving him the larger-than-life, Golden God appearance he seemed to relish.

Guerra had seen photographs of him in his briefing documents, and among those there were some moving images. But he looked so different as a young man, when his political and cultural revolution was also young.

Here, he was well-coiffed, short but dark-skinned and grim-looking, the kind of man one would expect to lead a whole people. His smile was coy and yet knowing, as though he held some vast private knowledge, and Guerra suspected that's what brought supporters flooding to his support.

It's how he came to dominate the ARK, Guerra thought.

"We are one," the projection of Dysart said. "We are the *true* ambassadors of humankind, and we deserve to reap the benefits of our heritage."

He paused, smiling, and then continued. "I have delivered you into a new age, have I not? I have identified our people's *true* enemy, have I not?"

The hologram flickered, but the sound persisted. Dysart said, "Do I *not* deserve your admiration, then? Your *loyalty*? Go ahead. Turn and look at your countrymen. *Look* at them."

There was a noticeable pause, and then the ship's leader continued.

"Can you, by looking at them, discern who is pure and who is not? If not, then *why* not? Because *you* have failed. You have failed to keep this ship pure, and you do not *value* your heritage. Our heritage. Most importantly, *my* heritage."

"This is awful," Sahana said.

"But effective," Sterling replied. "This is exactly what he *wanted*."

"So go ahead," Dysart continued, "go forth and ensure the perfection of our species. Of our people. Of our *race*."

Suddenly, the darkness in the room lifted, and the projector sputtering to a stop. The room was silent again.

"That was heavy," Katarina said.

"Crushing," Sterling replied.

Guerra glanced over and saw Coulson staring at the walls. He hadn't been paying attention—at all.

"Oh, hey—shit," he said. "What's this?"

29

Coulson was running his finger over something on the wall. It wasn't until the medic pointed it out that Guerra noticed it at all. He had gone sight blind to the gore and the filth of the ARK, and it told him he needed to pay more attention.

He couldn't afford to be sloppy. None of them could. Sloppiness meant death.

So Guerra shook off the yawning chasm of exhaustion and approached Coulson, who was peering at the wall as if he might fall through any second.

"What is it?" Guerra asked, and Coulson shrugged as he made room for the diplomatic officer.

It looked—*organic*.

A bluish moss—or something that might grow in the dank, forgotten corners of a ship.

It was *not* meant for the wide open, well-lit spaces within a ship. The thought that it was here—in this spot—gave Guerra a little half-heart attack.

This stuff was growing right out in the open, like it had every right to be here.

And the implication was not that it could grow anywhere, but that it had come from the *people* on the ship.

Guerra had no facts—no science—to back it up.

But he knew it to be true.

"Could be related to the experiments," Sahana said, as if reading his mind.

Guerra quietly said, "Or the thing crawling around in the depths of the ship."

"Or that," she said. "It's impossible to know, for sure. Unless Coulson's little machine can give us a clue as to what it is."

She looked closer.

"It's growing on the bodies," Sahana said, pointing to one of the figures suspended from the ceiling. "Looks like it might have originated there. Or spread from there."

Guerra squinted at it. "Have you seen it anywhere else?"

She shook her head. "Then again, I haven't been looking for it. It very well could have been everywhere."

"I'll test it," Coulson said.

After a brief lull, the machine lit up, and Coulson read the results.

His face twisted into something depressing.

"This stuff ain't human, either," he said, "so all I can tell you is that it comes from somewhere—or something—we humans just aren't familiar with."

A hush fell over the group.

"What does this mean?" Sterling asked the group. "I mean, really. On a fundamental level, what does this mean?"

No one spoke, but eventually, everyone turned to look at Guerra. He nodded sadly and laid it all out for them.

"It's not that simple," Guerra said. "The first thing that comes to mind is that—"

"Something alien invaded the ship," Sahana said.

Coulson nodded. "Fucking A."

Guerra gave that thought some breathing room. Even Katarina nodded at the prospect.

Then he said, "That might be true."

"The implication," Sterling added, "is that the raving lunatics dismantling this ship, piece by piece, are injecting themselves with these mods."

Guerra nodded, and a slow realization came over the group.

Sahana said, "If the mods are what's driving the people crazy, then it's the mods that contain the alien serum."

"Bingo."

Guerra stood back up—he'd been touching some of the blue stuff—and wiped his hands on his suit.

"Which means," he said, "that the Xenogradian government *knew* about what was coming in through their borders—and they did nothing to stop it."

"Stop it?" Coulson replied. "Looks like they fucking co-signed it. This is their grand accomplishment."

Guerra considered it.

"So they were bringing alien life forms aboard to test their modifications on? Is that the conclusion we're coming to?"

The rest of the group nodded.

"Seems about fucking right," Coulson said.

Sahana said, "And instead of strengthening their society through state-of-the-art chemistry, they destroyed it."

Sterling smiled wickedly. "The very definition of irony, am I right?"

Guerra didn't like the look of the kid's face, in that moment. There was something dark about his enjoyment of all the suffering.

"The remaining question is," Sahana said, "where did the alien life forms come from? And what *are* they?"

But before they could fully explore that idea, the doors at the end of the main floor lit up and opened, revealing a stairwell leading to the next area of the museum.

"Going up?" Coulson said, smiling.

"Guess so."

∼

On the second floor, they encountered more of the same lame attempts at brainwashing as they had on the first.

Coulson raised his middle finger at one of the videos, which featured Dysart standing before a crowd, shouting epithets and pounding his fists on the lectern.

"It's all 'outsiders did this' and 'outsiders did that.' He's just running the same old totalitarian playbook."

"Where there is no love and compassion," Sahana said, "hatred works best."

They stopped before the giant screen and watched the main thrust of Dysart's argument.

Dysart himself had prepared for this moment. His military cosplay was immaculate, down to the bristly, thick mustache.

And his face. There was something almost inhuman about it, though Guerra ultimately could not put his finger on it.

The proportions were all wrong, maybe. Misshapen eyes and doughy skin. He looked so much *older* than he had in the earlier video.

Of course, this was a campaign event. A rally, as it were, and surely he wanted to convey his strength and toughness to his constituents.

The man who had driven Xenograd to the brink leaned forward, mouth pressing into the mic, and said, "It's an obvious statement to say we all grew up in the ARK, right? Right. We all grew up here under this same roof, and we all worked, hand in glove, to make sure this place would be somewhere our kids would want to live. Isn't that what we want to continue on with, this belief in ourselves?"

A raucous cheer filled the speakers, and though there was joy in it, Guerra also thought he heard some viciousness, as well, as though the people—*patriots*, they would no doubt call themselves—had something to prove.

Or to purge.

Dysart, with his wide smile and giant hands, continued his speech, and even though Guerra hadn't heard it, he could surmise where it would go next.

"And yet," Dysart said, his voice booming in the speakers, "there are some among us who are thieves and traitors."

A collective gasp and a smattering of *boos* from the crowd.

"They are not breaking the locks on your sleep consoles, nor are they collaborating with a foreign agent, but nevertheless they are disintegrating the very foundation of Xenograd."

This time, the gasps could not be heard over the sound of angry screams.

He's whipping them into a frenzy, Guerra thought.

"These agents of destruction," Dysart continued, "they do not wear masks or hide their identities. No, no, no. No, these monsters—they are somehow worse. They hide in plain sight."

The camera cut to the figures in the stands. Their cries had reached a fever pitch, and the near-hysterical cries were accompanied by stomping and clapping and what could only be described as *gnashing of teeth*.

Dysart leaned toward the microphone again, pausing for just a few moments, just long enough for the crowd, lingering on his every word, to fall to a desperate and capricious silence.

"Do you want me to tell you who they are?" he asked.

The crowd erupted in a show of support.

Speaking above the group, he said, "Do you want me to name names?"

Again, the crowd replied in the affirmative, cheering and clapping as if their literal lives depended on it.

"Do you want me to be the one to stop these inhuman creatures?"

The sound allowed in by the microphones and pushed out by the speakers began to distort, as the cheers reached a seismic volume.

"Okay," he said, "settle down—settle down!—and I will tell you."

The crowd eventually did as he asked, and he waited patiently, taking time to wipe the sweat from his brow as he stood there in his military fatigues.

"The people," he said, pausing, drawing out every word or phrase for maximum impact, "are sitting...right next to you."

There was a moment of confusion, as the members of the crowd gasped and turned on one another, peering down their rows and behind them, trying to figure out just what in the world the presidential candidate could possibly be talking about.

"The traitors among us—please calm down—are *stowaways*. They are not our brethren, and they are not pure of blood. They *pretended* to be part of our culture, and they walk around as if they are, but I am here to tell you, they are *not*. They lie and cheat every day by not admitting just *who* they are."

The jeers coming from the crowd could almost be mistaken for animalistic cries, hyenas caught in bear traps or something similar. Either way, the noise did not sound human whatsoever.

"Would you like to see one of these...animals?"

The crowd gave an appreciable response, though it sounded much more like a growl than assent.

"Bring out the mixed blood," he said, almost off-mic, and then some goons dressed in hoods dragged a half-starving person out to center stage.

Guerra tried to see the victim, a woman whose face was blurred by the jumpy nature of the video.

Is that—is that *Beatrix*, he wondered.

His heart raced at the prospect. This place was so full of secrets, it was impossible to get any real information from the official channels.

But maybe, just maybe, if he could hang on and see this person, it could unlock some of the secrets about the nature of the ARK and its inhabitants.

The woman lifted her face and turned it toward the camera.

Here goes, Guerra thought.

The screen jittered, jumped, and then died.

∼

"I hate missing the ending to a movie," Coulson said, feigning disappointment.

"I think we all know how it ends," Sahana said.

"That's the *joke*," Coulson replied.

"This is nothing to joke about," Sahana said.

"Well, I didn't say it was *funny*," Coulson replied. "It's more like black humor. You know—gallows humor?"

"I think we may be too close to the gallows for humor, don't you?" Sahana replied, and Coulson went silent.

"Still," Guerra said, changing the topic, "it is amazing that they managed to capture the moment democracy died right on camera."

"Democracy died," Sahana said, "and The State was born."

"And we all suffer for it," Sterling added.

They followed the walkway through the next door and down a long hallway.

The hallway itself was covered in misleading posters denouncing the rest of the galaxy for foisting a "foreign horde" upon their people.

Guerra couldn't help but comment on it.

"It is heartbreaking to know that people are so easily manipulated by outright lies."

"Depends on how badly they want to believe it," Sahana said.

"The desire for belief can wipe out all reason, I agree," Guerra replied.

It reminded the diplomat of a time he'd rather forget, a time toward the end of his parents' lives.

When the paranoia took over.

They believed God was watching them directly, that He—in His Almighty wisdom—had stumbled upon two sinners parading around as the anointed.

And He was not happy.

There were beatings. There were scary nights, nights in which Guerra didn't sleep for fear that his mom and dad might do something irreversible to him.

The closet was the worst of it.

Oh, how he feared the closet.

Not unlike the walls of the museum, their closet was dotted with a fuzzy, incomprehensible mold.

The nights he wasn't allowed to sleep in his bed—when he was locked up and forgotten—he spent *hours* inspecting the black circles creating a pattern on the base of the walls.

"You all right, boss?"

Guerra looked to see Sterling walking alongside him. The kid's face had un-tensed, and he looked almost like one of the gang. Not at all like his parents had bought and paid his way into the UG.

"Yeah."

"You were talking to yourself," he said. "Mumbling. I just didn't—I thought maybe the rest of the group shouldn't hear it."

"Oh," Guerra replied, suddenly grateful. "I didn't know. I'm—"

"Don't apologize," he said. "I think everybody's going a little cuckoo in here."

"What do you mean?"

Sterling eyed him like he was making fun of the kid.

"Take a look at Katarina."

He did. The soldier was sauntering along—well ahead of them—her gun held tightly in her hands.

"I—I don't see it," Guerra responded.

"Look closer," Sterling said, "and you just might."

He did, and though he saw the same, stolid figure, he nodded a little bit. He didn't want to give the kid a complex.

Either Sterling was a little too paranoid—or Guerra wasn't paranoid enough.

"Sure—yeah."

"Right?" Sterling replied. "I think we're all going a little loony out here."

"How are you holding up?"

"Oh, I'm fine," he said. "Years of therapy, I guess. Sorry about freaking out back there. I'm just—this is a lot."

"Don't worry about it," Guerra said. "We've all been on our first mission before."

"Coulson hates me."

"Coulson hates *everybody*," Guerra said. "Don't think about him. It's just his nature."

Sterling paused, looking like he wanted to say something, and then went silent.

Then, Katarina jerked to a stop ahead of them.

"Wait a second," Katarina said, her voice barely above a whisper.

They all halted.

"Do you hear that?"

Katarina moved ahead, her footfalls silent as she sped to the end of the hall.

Once there, she turned and faced the group, tapping one ear with her index finger to indicate that they needed to listen.

They tiptoed to her, and they glanced down over her shoulder at the scene below them.

A group of hooded figures knelt in front of an elaborate statue of their Dear Leader, and they hummed an atonal song in somber reflection.

"I think they're—they're *worshipping* the statue."

"What? Like a God?"

"It appears so."

30

It looked like a makeshift memorial, complete with wilted flowers and effigies to the man who had directly placed all the people of Xenograd in this mess.

Not that much of anything made sense to Guerra, but this made *even less* sense to him.

"Be wary," he said, in response to his thoughts. "If these people are Dysart loyalists, they are likely hostile."

"Everything on this fucking ship is hostile," Coulson said, and Sterling nodded dolefully.

As they stepped closer, Guerra saw that the statue itself had been modified. Dysart's head and neck had been taken off completely, the shoulders polished to a smooth, brilliant shine.

The hands, too, had been polished so that the arms ended in blunt, tentacle-like protuberances.

On the Dysart statue's chest, the worshipers had carved a symbol. From a distance, it was a jumbled mess, but as they got closer, Guerra could see that it was a series of snake-like creatures spiraled around one central item: a stick or a sword or something like that.

The word *cult* was not likely to raise eyebrows in the insane bubble of violence the ARK had become, but Guerra was afraid of what this encounter might look like.

It was then that a shadowy thought crossed his mind.

Just take them out, his internal voice said. Just send them to whatever god they're praying to, and you can go about your business of getting *out* of this hellscape.

Guerra was about to clear his throat when the figures' chanting ceased, and the first of the robed figures turned to face the group.

"Get your weapons ready," Coulson whispered, but Guerra shook his head.

"Not yet," he said, implying he meant *not at all*.

Katarina, not surprisingly, held fast to her assault weapon, but the rest of the group heeded his command.

A low, resonant voice erupted from the circle of prayer-bound people and stopped them in their tracks.

"Do you bend the knee," the voice said, "or will you bend the neck?"

"We don't mean you any harm," Guerra said. "Actually, we were—"

"Just passing through?"

"Well," Guerra said. "Yeah."

The hooded folk stood as one and turned to face Guerra and his shell-shocked crew.

It was then Guerra noticed their faces.

If the modders were addicts—or if they were mutated humans—these people had the same thing.

Their faces were slight exaggerations of normal human faces.

And their eyes—their eyes were *yellow*. Like someone had poured neon light into their pupils.

"My name," he said, "is Okudah. I am one of the remaining members of The Sect to survive the ousting. We all are."

Each group nodded at the other, and then several moments of awkward silence passed among them.

Then, Guerra asked, "What are *their* names?"

Okudah's eyes cut sideways toward his group. Then he said, "Oh, they prefer not to speak. It is a contract they have made with the God-King."

Okudah, tall and lithe and dark-skinned, motioned to the crew and said, "Follow me. We can talk as we traverse the path of the museum."

"Is it—is it safe?" Sterling asked. "Because some of the things we've encountered—"

"Have been taken care of here in the museum," Okudah said. "Ironically enough, the museum is probably the place with the most actual life on the whole ship."

"Well, that's good," Sterling said, not sounding entirely convinced.

As they passed the statue, Guerra—and presumably the others—got a good look at it.

Okudah seemed to notice, and a knowing, almost empathetic smile crossed his face.

"That is a symbol of our faith," he said. "It is the—"

"The Leviathan," Guerra said, meeting Okudah's gaze.

The man's reaction was one borne of respect.

"Close," he said. "We call it the Behemoth, but the idea is the same. It is an avatar of our beliefs."

"And what *are* those beliefs?" Sahana asked.

Okudah nodded. "It is the result of a series of cataclysmic events aboard the ship. They exposed the wicked, the corrupt, and they crystalized our ideas about the end of the world. Which, I guess, is the ship."

"What were those events?"

They reached a door—a security checkpoint—and Okudah scanned an ID pass for someone was most certainly dead before answering.

"It's a more complicated story than that," he replied, "so forgive me if I have to wind around a few things before we reach the conclusion."

"I think we're okay with that."

Guerra looked back at the group as they walk, and the crew nodded.

Coulson shrugged. "I'm just happy not to be chased by those half-human monsters out there."

"Speaking of," Sterling asked, "can you start with the existence of the Kharisiri?"

Okudah glared at him with yellow eyes.

"No," Guerra said. "Those aren't who—he means the people, er, *not* from this ship."

"Ah. The *stowaways*," Okudah replied.

"Right," Guerra said.

The monk nodded softly. "It's believed that the tragedy of the ARK can be traced back to a family that hid aboard the ship as it took off. They managed to infiltrate Xenograd and reproduce, thus muddying the waters of who belonged on the ship."

"Why do you care about something so trivial?" Sahana asked.

"This is *our* ship," he said. "Our families earned the right to be on the ARK—to repopulate Xenograd—and to us, it is unfair, at the least, to instigate oneself into our midst."

"Where they came from seems like a trivial point."

"*Billions* of human beings perished after we left," Okudah said. "We left them behind. We abandoned them, so that we could continue on—continue the business of being human."

"Right," Coulson replied.

He sounded skeptical, but the monk seemed to ignore the tone in the medic's voice.

"It is not a trivial point," he said, doubling down. "Not to me. Not to anyone who lived on our Sister Earth, either."

Sahana would not let the point go.

"But purity—"

"Purity is not the issue here," Okudah said, and he said it in a way that seemed to make it a final point.

Sahana opened her mouth for a rebuttal—Guerra himself even remembered the quibble about blood purity earlier—but he caught the mystic's eyes and shook his head.

Thankfully, she demurred.

There would be time to legislate all of this at some future point.

But that point was not now.

"Is it possible—and this is me just trying to put things together—that they came from *somewhere else*?"

Okudah stared blankly ahead, his face a mask of unsympathetic disinterest.

"In the end," he said, "it does not matter."

"No," Guerra clarified, "I mean, what if—what if the *stowaways* you're talking about—what if they came from out there? In space?"

Fear flashed across the monk's face, and it took him a moment to get that part of himself under control.

"I believe we're getting to the heart of the matter," he said. "This is where the leap of logic requires some stretching."

"No offense, fella," Coulson replied, "but I think we're about fucking ready for anything, at this point."

Okudah took that in silently, and after a time he nodded.

"You've seen the modification stations littered throughout Xenograd, yes?"

Guerra nodded. "Absolutely," he said. "They promise to make you run faster, jump higher—"

"And fuck better," Coulson finished.

"Anyway," Guerra said. "Yes, we have."

"Those modifications—at first, they were seen as a revolution for the Xenogradian people."

"And then?"

"And then—things started to change."

"Yeah, no shit."

Guerra glared at Coulson, but it did nothing to shame him.

"No one asked any questions, because everyone was enamored with what they were capable of. It was like humanity was taking a giant leap forward, and we had a monopoly on it."

"What was the prevailing belief around the, um, *stowaways* at the time?"

Okudah almost seemed to dismiss the question. Then, he said, "The...distaste for them was growing. It had not hit an apex yet, but paranoia was rampant around the ship."

"And then?"

"Then, the graffiti started showing up, and that's when people began questioning where the mods were coming from."

"The Beatrix stuff?"

Okudah shook his head. "No, that would come later. In the beginning, it was just guerrilla marketing, of a sort."

"Which means?"

"It would be these short phrases spray painted on store fronts or on the sides of buildings."

"And so how does that relate to what happened here?" Guerra asked. "To Dysart himself? And Beatrix?"

"There was a silent civil war between the loyalists and the splinter group. Violence never spilled out into the streets until—"

"Until Beatrix."

Okudah nodded. "She was the model of everything wrong with the ship, or at least we thought so."

"Because she came from somewhere else?"

Okudah sneered. "Nationalism is strong *everywhere*," he said, "but *especially* here on the ARK. I don't apologize for it, because it has brought us great favor."

"Oh yeah," Coulson said, "like a zombie apocalypse."

"I don't remember how—or when," Okudah continued, "but at some point it became insinuated among the Xenogradian people that the mods were the result of genetic human testing."

He let that settle in, and then he continued.

"And somehow the idea that children were being used as test subjects began making the rounds, and people stopped using mods. They thought they were injecting the blood of stowaways."

"Turns out," Guerra said, "they were injecting an alien substance."

"Who knows how things might have turned out, had we found *that* out in the lead-up to the riots."

"But that's true."

"That the stuff for the mods came from…elsewhere? Your guess is as good as mine."

"It's actually *not* a guess," Coulson said, "because the samples I tested—"

"Your samples could be wrong," Okudah said. "At some point, *everything* on this ship has been proven exactly correct or exactly wrong."

Coulson only smirked to himself.

But Okudah was not done. He and his minions walked in a tight pack of worshippers, and he whispered something to the one standing next to him before continuing.

"In an effort to quell the uprising, Dysart proposed injecting himself with a plethora of mods right in front of everyone—on camera."

"And then what happened?"

"He...changed."

"Changed how?"

Okudah's eyebrows raised into a expression indicating a capacity for surprise.

"I'm sure you've heard the sound of the creature lurking somewhere in the ARK."

31

Guerra felt the world shift underneath him. It was like the ground in the ARK had transformed into chewed bubble gum.

"Whoa, whoa," Coulson said. "You're not saying—he's not saying—"

"That's *exactly* what I'm saying," Okudah confirmed. "The beast that roams the ship *is* Commander General Dysart—in the flesh."

It didn't make sense—none of it made sense—but he had someone from the ship—actually from Xenograd—telling him this, so it was almost like he had no choice *but* to believe it.

Coulson looked like a man who had just been told he was a ghost. "So let me get this straight: the whale-sounding beast thumping around on this ship is your Dear Leader, turned into a goddamned space monster?"

Guerra allowed that point to sink in before continuing. He glanced over at Okudah, whose face was implacable, filled with the kind of self-satisfaction only a true believer can possess.

"So now that he's a literal monster—rather than a metaphorical one—you've decided to *worship* him?"

Okudah's smile became dark with venom. There was the minutest gap between his two front teeth, on what was otherwise a pristine face.

"It isn't what he *is*," he said, "but what he has *become* that pleases us. He is still essentially human, but—"

"He is more human than human," Sahana finished.

Guerra couldn't believe his ears.

And yet, here they were, taking in this moment.

"I see the look you're giving me," Okudah continued, "but what you must understand before you judge is that this man—surely a fraud to outsiders like yourselves—actually managed to accomplish the thing we all strove to do. The peak we all attempted to reach."

"He transformed himself," said Sahana.

Okudah nodded. "Some out there tried desperately, and they reaped insanity or death for their efforts. But he—Dysart—managed to become the ruler of all rulers."

"Speaking of the—the *stowaways*—out there, why aren't you like them? How did you manage to remain, well, *sane*?"

"We are the chosen few. The only ones to *survive*."

"Yes, but how? Does it have something to do with—what did you call it—the *ousting*?"

The robed priest nodded. "While it is true that Dysart injected himself with a new formula, he asked us—his *people*—to mirror the activity. To inject ourselves with a similar mod to prove our allegiance."

Sahana said, "And you chose not to?"

With that question, Okudah actually laughed. It was a booming, throaty gesture, and it put Guerra on edge.

"There was no such thing as *choice*," he said. "Dysart made sure of that. Besides, no one in Xenograd would choose such a thing. They were all loyal to *him*."

"Not everybody," Coulson replied, tapping a bit of graffiti on the walls.

"That's true. Many people believe the batch was poisoned, that the outsiders laced it with an alien chemical to do—to change everyone in that irreversible, fundamental way."

"Do you believe that?"

"I believe everything happens for a reason," he replied. "I do not bother with the *why*. Only the outcome. And that's why we're escorting you now."

"And why is that?"

The monk said, "You are not my *enemy*. We worship our God-King, and he protects us. We do not need protection from you and your kind, do we?"

"No," Guerra said. "We're diplomats, not warriors."

"Then you have nothing to fear from *us*," Okudah replied.

Guerra thought about that, then nodded.

"So—what," Guerra asked, returning to the previous subject. "You all injected yourselves, and you didn't become monsters. Is that it?"

"Faith relies upon reality," he said, "and how you experience it."

Guerra wasn't satisfied with the question, so he asked it again.

"If Dysart injected himself—"

"Which he did," Okudah interrupted.

"—Then shouldn't you all be...like *him*?"

"We are alive because of Dysart," he said. "We are protected because of Dysart. We are human because of Dysart. That is all that matters to me."

Guerra felt conversation's door being shut, so he left it at that, at least for a little while. They settled into a silent rhythm, until Sterling tugged on Guerra's suit.

The kid whispered, "The way we're going—it doesn't line up with my map. We're going far afield of where the comms station is supposed to be."

Guerra considered it, then said, "This is the path of least resistance. Once we get to wherever they're taking us, we can go our own way if they're giving us the flim-flam."

Sterling "What if it's to—I don't know—slaughter us and harvest our organs?"

"They don't even have *weapons*, Sterling. And if they pull something, we have Katarina on our side."

He was trying to project confidence, but Guerra felt the pang of discontent and uncertainty all the way down in his bowels.

The crew already thought he was weak. If he called for them to turn around or pull away now, they'd almost certainly lose all faith in him—maybe even mutiny.

The alternative was for him to let them be led to their doom, all because he didn't want to take a stand in a difficult situation.

So he decided to split the difference.

He hurried up to the front of the group and shouldered up beside Okudah.

"My guide says we're way off-track here," Guerra said, "and I don't want to step on your—you know—hospitality or whatever, but I've got to know why."

"Why what?"

"Why are we so far from the comms station?"

"Your—your *guide* told you we were far away?"

"Yes."

"If he were guiding you, how did you end up in the museum?" Okudah asked. "It is nowhere near the comms station. Not even close."

"But—"

"Listen, I don't want to tell you your business, but your man is flat-out wrong."

Guerra steeled himself, but he felt like his insides were on fire.

"I, uh—I think I should go talk to him," Guerra said. "He's a new guy, and so maybe he got turned around."

Okudah shrugged. "Whatever you decide, it's up to you," he said. "But *this* is the way to the comms station."

"He's fucking—he's *lying!*" Sterling said, when Guerra stepped back to speak with him. "Let me share you on my screen, and I can show you exactly—"

"You *are* new at this," Guerra said, by way of explanation. "It's entirely understandable if you—"

"I didn't make a mistake," Sterling replied. "He's honey-potting us, leading us to our doom. I think we—"

"Hold it," said a voice from up front. "We're here."

Guerra cut Sterling off with a wave of the hand and hurried up to where the members of The Sect were standing.

"Tell your people to be on their toes," Okudah said, once they reached the end of the tunnel underneath the museum.

"Why is that?"

The priest's smirk returned. "Because we're in a green zone. Once you step out into the midst of the ship, you're on your own. And it's *hellish* out there."

Guerra looked at him, and the man seemed honest. As honest as anybody he'd encountered on this or any other ship. Guerra might not be much of a leader, but he thought he was one hell of a judge of character.

"All right," Guerra said. "Let's get to it."

"Once we get to the other side of the gate, I'll point you in the direction of the comms station. But you're on your own after that. Let's get it open."

One of the other monks flipped a switch, and the entire wall began to rise.

And then something occurred to Guerra, something he didn't quite know was necessary to ask until just now.

"Why would you do this?" he asked. "Why would you help us, if you're—I don't know—loyalists for the Dysart regime?"

"It's like I told you," he said, smiling, "everything happens for a reason. And since we crossed paths, I thought it was a sign."

"You did?"

"Everything is a sign. Everything has a consequence. And, ultimately, absolutely everything is done in order to—"

But Okudah didn't get to finish that thought, because that moment was when absolutely everything went to complete hell.

32

By the time the gate was fully up, they—the modders, the stowaways, the Kharasiri, whatever—had flooded the small lobby at far end of the museum.

They were loud, growling creatures, some stumbling and gibbering as they approached, but others…others moved as gracefully as dancers landing a series of very aggressive moves.

"Fall back!" Katarina screamed, raising her rifle and firing a precise burst of gunfire into the middle of the crowd.

Several heads popped open like coffins left to rot, and bright geysers of blood shot fountain-high into the air above them. It might have been somewhat beautiful, were it not so blatantly horrific.

Its intended purpose—to frighten their attackers into turning tail and running away—failed miserably. Instead of hesitation, the lunatic fringe of Xenograd's population showed utter aggression in return. They stepped over—or directly on top of—their comrades and just kept coming.

It was the death march of a thousand enraged devils of Xenograd, all descending upon them in a single cataclysmic event.

"Don't wait on my command," Guerra said suddenly. "Fire when ready. Save yourselves."

And so they did. They raised their weapons and turned the force to full power. It was usually only acceptable to use as a means for dispersing large crowds during riots—from a distance.

Up close, rounds from the force gun would be devastating to the lives and limbs of anyone who was unfortunate enough to come into contact with them.

They fired, fired, fired again.

The blasts of air, severe as they were, did nothing to slow the advance of the crowd.

Even when limbs were ripped free of the sockets, they kept coming, spilling a horrid-smelling blood openly on the floor around them—but persisting, nevertheless.

It was a scene of gruesome horror Guerra hadn't imagined in his worst nightmares.

But that's not true, is it? the voice inside him said.

He was reminded of the thoughts and images he was provided by his numerous forced readings of Revelation, in which the sky became as dark as sack cloth and the seas ran with blood.

The museum's exit wasn't exactly black as sack cloth—as Revelation suggested—but the emergency lights only cast a dim, blue pallor over the long, high-ceilinged room, so it was close enough.

And the river of blood—that was obvious. The brightly colored blood was something of a puddle at this point, if not an out-and-out river, flowing through the hallways.

He was knocked out of his momentary fugue by Coulson screaming across the hall at him.

"Guerra! Get your fucking head out of your ass and help us fight this goddamned plague!"

Plague, he thought, and his heart thumped in his chest.

Then, all at once, sound and sight and smell came to him, and he flicked the switch on his force gun to full bore. The hum of the charge in his hand was like holding pure electricity, and he let it all—including his hatred for this situation—flow through him.

He pulled the trigger and was nearly knocked flat on his ass by the blast of kinetic energy.

But the effect of it was immediate and apparent. The bodies of two attackers exploded, the concussive force of his gun dismembering the frothing attackers limb by bloody limb. The head and arms and legs and torso all went flying in separate directions, sending blood in a gruesome spray across the remaining horde.

And yet, the creatures just kept coming. They couldn't be deterred or frightened like human antagonists, and death only seemed to stoke the fires of their rage.

Then, his heart started racing, and though he fought the instinct to run, something fundamental and horrifying occurred to him.

"It's not enough," he said to himself, and then to the rest of the group. "It's not enough!"

"Yeah, no shit!" Coulson screamed back. "Unless you have a brilliant idea jammed square up your ass, we're all going to be celebrated with posthumous honors at the UG."

They all looked as worried as he felt. Even Katarina, the very picture of stalwart determination, seemed to be fraying at the edges.

Something had to be done, and he guessed that distinction had descended upon him.

He backed away, lowering his weapon, and the rest of them took notice.

Coulson—as expected—was the first to speak up.

"You can't chicken out now, asshole," he screamed. "We're all in this suicide pact *together*."

He glanced around him and then got an idea that, if not brilliant, was at least *different*.

"I'll be right back," he said, pulling away from the group and running back toward the museum's interior.

He reached an abandoned little shop he'd noticed on the way over, and he kicked in the storefront's giant front pane of glass. It shattered with a satisfying, chaotic tinkle of glass, and then he was inside.

Guerra was looking for something specific, and he shouted when his eyes landed on the object of his search.

The sign above the exit read:

THANK YOU
WE HOPE YOU'VE ENJOYED
THE MUSEUM.
FEEL FREE TO SAMPLE
A MODIFICATION.

Guerra's mind turned it over, and then he acted. He didn't have time to ponder whether or not injecting alien plasma into himself was a good idea or not.

The choice had been made for him.

They were coming, and they were hungry.

He looked over the options and decided upon the one that seemed most fitting for the situation.

BRAIN BULLET

It was a silly name, but it seemed to translate to exactly what he was looking for.

He pounded the button below it, and moments later a small vial with a minuscule needle popped out of the vending machine.

With a flick of the wrist, he brought the tiny syringe down into his arm and thumbed the plunger.

The effect was *immediate.*

His whole body began to shake as if suffering some heinous form of epilepsy.

His veins burned like they had been injected with acid, and he struggled to hold himself upright.

But he did. He kept his feet on the ground, and his head about six-and-a-half feet above that, because he knew if he didn't, he would lie down and die.

He didn't know how he knew that, but he did.

He knew it as well as he knew that what he had just done to himself was irreversible.

After about a minute of white-hot pain, he was able to stand upright and listen to the increasingly desperate screams of his teammates back at the museum's exit.

But there was one thing he couldn't quite get past, and he thought about it while he trekked back to the fight.

While he was in the throes of his pained...*evolution*, he had this vision. It was a strange, out-of-body experience, but one he thought everyone who took these mods probably went through the first time.

He felt a rush in which he could actually *see* the fluid from the syringe coursing through his body. It wasn't that he could imagine it; no, he could fucking *see* it.

And in that moment—that brief flash of time—he saw, as his father put it, "all of Heaven and Earth, with Hell beneath it."

He saw what he could only think of as a living embodiment of death. Death Itself, he might say.

It was a ragged shard of darkness that had a life force, and even though he couldn't see its features, he knew they were there.

And just being in its presence sent him into paroxysms of fear.

When he shook free of it, he could feel a hot wetness down in the crotch of his suit. The fear had overwhelmed him, and there was still the silhouette of a monster submerged deep in his conscious mind.

But he would have to deal with that later.

For now, he had to fend off a semi-mindless horde.

He hurried back to the scene of the battle, and things weren't looking good. The stowaways—as Okudah called them—had crested the largest barrier to entry. It was a blockade of tables and chairs from the nearby food court, and it was a paltry excuse for protection.

There was a whole mass of blood and bodies on the floor, but those that were uninjured—or modestly injured—were still coming.

And they were close.

"The fuck have you *been*?" Coulson asked him, but Guerra didn't wait to respond.

"Hold your fire," he said, feeling this new power surging through him as he stepped ahead of them.

"Why in the hell would we do that?" Coulson asked, but Guerra only held one hand up to stop his talking.

They ceased their shooting, and in that moment, Guerra closed his eyes, the only sound in that room the chaos of approaching death.

Guerra got a mental glimpse of the creature he'd seen after the injection, and he felt his pulse quicken. His heart thudded a beat against his chest, and then the next moment, something happened.

His head was thrust back with the force of a shotgun blast that rattled his eardrums and sent a blinding, scorched earth pain through his eye sockets.

But then—then, there was just silence.

33

He looked up, his eyes blurry with the force of what he'd just done, and saw the outcome.

Every single person—stowaway, Xenogradian, modder, whatever—lay in a puddle of blood and gore.

A few began to moan, but it was the sound of something going quickly to ground. None of them had very much time left, and Guerra knew it. *They* had to know it, too.

"Wow," Coulson said from beside him. "Just—fucking *wow*."

Out of the mass of carcasses on the floor, a small object slithered into view, and it quickly became apparent that it was a slug or a worm of some kind.

"The fuck are *those*?" Coulson asked.

"*Those*," Okudah said, "are what cause everyone in this ship—low-born Xenogradian and stowaway alike—to go wild, to wreck everything in sight."

"And where do they come from?" Guerra asked, feeling his voice catch in his throat.

But Okudah didn't answer, and it was then Guerra knew. He didn't have to be told where all of it was headed.

He was a ticking clock, and the biological timer inside him had just been set.

"What was that?" Sahana asked. "How did you—"

"It was the fucking mod, wasn't it?" Coulson asked. "You just injected yourself with alien juice. How does that shit feel?"

"I don't know," Guerra said. "I mean, is that how it's supposed to work?"

Okudah looked astonished. "That mod was made for men and women looking to protect their homes. Think *pistol* fired from the center of your frontal lobe."

Surveying the carnage around them, Sterling said, "I think this goes far *beyond* how it's supposed to work."

Guerra didn't know how to take that, but he felt a powerful unease spreading through his vital organs.

There was a quiet joy in the air around them, and though the crew wasn't smiling, they had to be happy with this outcome.

Even the Dysart-worshipping monks seemed at peace with this result.

At what price, Guerra thought.

It was like the video of his life had stopped, mid-frame, with him contemplating the nature of his existence.

Almost at once, the video restarted, and everybody began piling out of the museum.

Everybody but Guerra.

Okudah was the only one to notice his apprehension.

He walked up and clapped Guerra on both shoulders with his massive hands. There was a beatific smile stretched plainly across his face.

"Remember what I told you," he said, beaming. "Everything happens for a reason. *This* happened for a reason."

They followed the monk outside the museum and headed up a hill toward the highest point in this part of Xenograd.

The ground rumbled beneath their feet. Okudah stopped and stood there, ramrod straight.

"He's close," the monk said.

"Sounds like that scares you. Don't you want to see your dear God-King?"

"You are a Christian, yes?" Okudah asked.

Guerra was taken aback. "Not in many—how did you know that?"

"What does it say in your Christian Bible about looking upon the face of God?"

"Man is not equipped to—for a variety of reasons. For a time there, God didn't even like people making images of Him."

"Well, perhaps you *can* understand my apprehension then."

Okudah's fellow worshippers had fallen far behind, as if the act of walking had become untenable for them.

"Your friends back there," Guerra asked the priest, "are they going to be all right?"

"They are very devout," Okudah responded. "They haven't been outside the museum since it happened."

"It?"

"The Ousting," the monk said.

"Well," Guerra said, "I've been playing catch-up with all of the mystique surrounding this place, so you're going to have to remind me."

"In due time," Okudah said. "Right now, let's get you inside that communications station."

He stopped at the outer gate of a building that stretched high into the darkness of the ship.

"This is it," Okudah announced. "The comms station."

"All right!" Coulson yelled. "This is our fucking ticket *out* of here. Let's go."

Okudah's face turned dubious. He reached out and shook the gate's main opening.

Nothing happened.

"It's fucking *locked*?" Coulson asked.

"I'm afraid so," Okudah said.

Guerra felt his stomach turn to pure acid.

"You're kidding," he said.

Okudah's attention turned upward. The gate itself was as high as some buildings, and so climbing it was a non-starter.

Katarina stepped back and fired at the building, but it didn't do much of anything but make noise.

"That's not going to work," Okudah said. "This was a prized structure for Dysart and his government—"

"Yeah, until he decided to stop communicating with the outside world," Guerra said.

Okudah seemed confused at that. "What do you mean?"

"Just what I said," Guerra replied. "Xenograd was famously uncommunicative with other ships, in general, and the UG, in particular."

"That can't be," Okudah said.

"They were stripped from their position on the Security Council a *long* time ago."

"But Dysart always told us—he always said we had been forsaken by the other ships at-large."

"He fed you shit and told you it was bran flakes," Coulson said. "Happens to the best of us. That's how my last marriage ended."

The other monks had perked up at that last admission—the one about Dysart, not Coulson's marital woes—and Okudah fought to keep his feet.

It was like he'd been punched in the gut.

Guerra was glad someone stepped in to change the subject.

"Is there another way in?" Sahana asked. "I'm fairly good at climbing, if that's necessary."

Okudah shook his head, though his mind still seemed to be cogitating on Guerra's previous announcement. "Not that I'm aware of," he said.

"Huh," Guerra said.

After a moment, Coulson replied with, "Maybe we can ask the kid about an alternative path. Hey—uh—Sterling, can you—"

But the request died a fairly quick death in his throat, as he turned and saw that the new guy was nowhere to be found.

There was a momentary show of looking around, but it was clear he'd gone AWOL—or worse.

"Where'd you think he ran off to?" Coulson asked.

"I don't think he ran off at all," Sahana replied, her voice containing a grim warning. "I think the darkness of this ship swallowed him whole."

"Enough," Guerra said, peering into the darkness for any sign of the kid.

It was the poor bastard's first mission, and this was how it had turned out. Guerra was not one to play the political game at the UG, but he knew losing a major political figure's son in a wreck of a ship was no way to advance one's career.

"We've got to go find him," Guerra said.

Even as he said it, though, he felt himself fighting the idea. It would be *suicide* to go back the way they had come.

What if they angered another hornet's nest of those *things*?

His mind interjected, Well, you have a way of fighting them off now, don't you, you mental shotgun?

But he didn't listen to it.

Instead, he tried to put everybody back on the level.

"Before we try to make a run for the comms station," Guerra said, "we've got to find Sterling."

"No," Coulson replied. "We are *here. He* wandered off—"

"We don't know that," Sahana commented.

"But *still*," Coulson said, his face a swirling mass of contempt, "he knows where we are. He's got the map. If he wants to get off this miserable hunk of crazy, he can tiptoe on over to where we are."

"What if he's in trouble?"

"Then he can get himself out."

"Coulson," Sahana said, "it's his *first mission*. He's—"

But Coulson was ready for that one.

"Oh, come on," he said. "He's a big boy. This is his first mission, but he knew the risks."

Everyone looked at him in a kind of shocked horror.

Coulson rolled his eyes. "I'm not saying we let the little fucker die, but it's like that old philosophical problem. The one with the lever. Do we let the train hit *one* of us, or do we pull the lever and potentially shift the tracks so that it runs *us* over?"

Then, there was a loud sound, as if someone flipping a huge power switch, and the whole ship hummed with a newfound energy, an energy Guerra and the rest of them had not experienced.

And a voice came over the speakers above them, as unmistakeable as it was horrifying.

It was like listening to Lazarus, back from the dead.

"Enough *fucking around*," the voice said. "Let's get right down to business, shall we?"

It was General Commander Dysart, sounding very much like himself and *not* the Leviathan stalking around the depths of the ship.

"Tell your monk there," Dysart said, "*I am risen.*"

"He is risen, indeed," Okudah said, his voice full of awe and reverence. "I—I can't believe this is true."

"Well," Coulson said, "fucking believe it, because that's the asshole's voice going over the loudspeakers, and it ain't no recording."

They all looked up at the ceiling, as if Dysart actually were speaking from the rafters of the ship, somewhere off in the distance.

Then, Dysart's voice boomed over the speakers again. It said, "I thought maybe we would have some fun, but I'm already bored with this. Get ready, *intergalactic diplomats.*"

There was only raw, unmitigated contempt in the disembodied voice.

"Time to die."

∼

TO BE CONTINUED...

JOIN THE NEWSLETTER—GET AN EXTENDED SAMPLE!

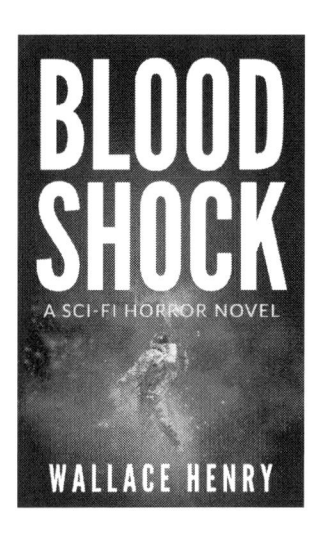

You've just finished the first volume of a four-part sci-fi horror series. Thank you! If you want to receive a free, extended sample of the next volume, Blood Shock, then click on the link below and get started!

Join the newsletter:

https://mailchi.mp/5ad656741e72/bloodshock

Printed in Great Britain
by Amazon